Accidental Destination

Accidental
Destination

ISBN: 978-0-9909729-0-7

The following is a work of fiction.
All characters and scenes are products of the author's imagination or are used fictitiously. Any resemblance to actual persons, places or events is purely coincidental.

Second printing

**This novel is not available on
stereo 8 track or cassette tapes.**

3536 Orchard Ave.
Saint Louis, Missouri 63074
www.coolwaypress.com
info@coolwaypress.com

ACCIDENTAL DESTINATION

a novel

Alex Balogh

DEDICATION:

For María Teresa, my half orange, as always, TQM;

For those intrepid travelers, wherever they may be,
who pulled up roots & lit out for parts unknown;

For the Emeralds of this world, those transitory
way stations, still flickering in our hearts,
minds & consciousness.

Trust the flow Joe
whatever you did is done
whatever you had is gone
you'll never find
  what's left behind
yet today's new sun
  is the same old one
& the waves you've begun
  keep moving on

Trust the flow Joe

Michael Castro

CONTENTS

THE ANTHILL

Jason dared not count what was left of his cash. He had walked straight from the bus station through a neighborhood of respectable enough houses, until he turned left into an unpaved alley and found himself staring up at a two-story monstrosity with peeling paint, sagging gutters and crumbling foundation. This couldn't possibly be the place.

Even in this unlit alley, the moon threw off enough light for Jason to make out both the house number and the address penciled on the scrap of paper he held in his hand. This was the place all right, but he hadn't expected such a rat hole.

He exhaled slowly, unsure of what was he doing here, in Emerald, in front of this house, this accidental destination, 3,000 miles and three days from the only home he had ever known. Maybe it was the lure of the unknown wilds that beckons gypsies, adventurers, artists and malcontents. Emerald was west of the West of the starlit prairies and cowboy coffee of his childhood fantasies and even further west (and much further north) into an America of unravaged land and unchartered vistas. It promised freedom from the congestion of tollways, buildings reaching for the sky, and slow suffocation from the concrete and sarcasm.

Emerald wasn't the San Francisco of his magazine musings, but he had never been to San Francisco, and the scene here had to be better than the neon glamour, dis-ease and unrest back East. Here he would smooth out the dissonance of his former life. Here he would bloom organic, far from the hustle and blare.

Maybe this is all a pipe dream, he thought, a rationalization, the result of a hastily mumbled prayer, but I had to get away and—whatever this is—it's my best chance yet, even if it ends up being nothing more than an illusion born of itchy feet, smoke and hazy promises.

The wooden railing wobbled when he grabbed it. He slung his backpack over his shoulder, tightened his grip on his guitar case, walked up the seven concrete steps to the front door, took a deep breath and knocked. It opened, and a bearded man with wide eyes that didn't blink and glasses opaque from grime stared right through him. The man was wearing a flannel shirt and jeans so dingy and caked with dirt that they were unrecognizable as any shade of denim. He held a Red Wing work boot in one hand and a polishing rag in the other. The boots looked like the most expensive things he could possibly own. Saying nothing, the man, who Jason would later come to know as Vodka, stepped aside and motioned for him to enter.

The front room was dim, lit only by a single candle burning atop a saucer, but Jason could make out two threadbare couches with stuffing erupting from their arms, a couple of well-worn upholstered chairs and a coffee table obscured by magazines, bottles and an ashtray overflowing with sunflower seed husks and burnt matches. A batik sheet, about the size of a tablecloth, hung on one wall. A dusty, wrinkled print of an Indian slumped on a horse was thumbtacked to another. The caption read: "The End of the Trail." A shirtless man tapped on a hand drum, a woman sat on a guy's lap, sharing a joint, listening to two others argue about how you had to *tuck em n fuck em* when there's that much *slash*. They glanced curiously at Jason or else paid him no attention at all.

Jason took another deep breath. "I'm looking for Tim."

Jason had never met Tim and knew nothing about him, except that he played guitar, he was cool and he lived here.

Tim was no more than a name to Jason, a friend of someone's friend who'd have a place for him to crash.

"Maybe Rusty's seen him," Vodka replied. "He's upstairs somewhere. Hey—Rusty!" Vodka yelled. "Some guy's here lookin' for Tim." Vodka nodded toward the stairs. "Go on up." Jason climbed the steps, which curved sharply to the left, and stood at the head of a hallway so deep that he couldn't see to the end.

A thin, balding man at least twice Jason's age stepped out of the darkness. "Tim's gone for a few days. Workin' the State Fair up north—Won't be back for another week—Heey, you just in from somewhere? Need a room? Yesirree—We've got one right here."

Without waiting for a response, he pushed open the first door on the left and stepped in. "As you can see, we've got it all—electricity—running water—there's even a bathroom down the hall." Rusty cracked his knuckles. "We're a cooperative household," he added as if everyone knew what a co-operative household was. Jason didn't yet know what a batik was. "There are sign-up sheets for kitchen and bathroom duties. We all share the one fridge. Whadaya think?" He spit out the words like a carnival barker.

Jason eyed the room. A makeshift bed, hammered together from plywood discards and 2x4 scraps, held up a foam pad covered with a sheet and a blanket. He looked out the window at the roof of the house across the alley. Air rippled around a steelpipe chimney. A month's rent was about what three nights in a motel would run, and he didn't have that kind of money to burn. His back ached, his neck was sore and that foam pad looked like a canopy bed at the Honolulu Hilton.

"Sure," he replied. "I'll take it."

Jason counted out the cash and handed it to Rusty, who folded the bills in half and stuck them in his T-shirt pocket, barely giving them a glance. "Welcome to The Anthill," he said. "You might want to get a padlock for your door, but folks rarely lock up. There's always someone around and the front door's always open." He turned and headed back down the hall. There was no conferring with other house members, no introductions and no receipt.

Jason sat on the bed and dangled his feet off the edge. He could still feel the vibration of the bus crawling along at 55 miles an hour from some small town to another fast-food burger joint. Life on the road was nothing like that crinkled paperback he had left on the bus. Not for him anyway. But things had to be better here. They had to be.

CULTURE SHOCK

Jason opened his eyes as the sun crept in through the bare window. It gets light earlier here, he thought as he rummaged through his backpack and pulled out a small box of raisins, the last of his provisions. He needed breakfast, but first, he needed his coffee. He pulled on his last clean pair of blue jeans—the ones he had been saving for this very occasion—and tiptoed down the squeaky stairs to the now-empty front room.

The air was stale and thick. Where did all those people go? he asked himself. I wonder how many of them actually live here. They all looked like they belong here, but this place can't possibly sleep them all, can it?

Jason pulled the front door open and stood on the landing, breathing in the crisp July air. I doubt I'll find any diners around here, he thought. I'll try that hippie joint—the one painted in those psychedelic colors—I saw last night near the bus station. I bet that place is a trip. He turned left and slowly walked the seven blocks south. Everything looked so different from what he was used to—the street signs, the houses with sheets covering the windows, the bushes, trees and plants springing up unbidden, scattered throughout the front yards and grassy strips next to the streets.

A tree—right here in town—hung low with cherries.

Maybe I can snag some of these later, he thought. He walked another half block and saw a tree loaded with purple fruit. *Are those plums!?* He pulled one off the tree and squeezed it. It wasn't ripe yet, but that wasn't the point. Jason wiggled his toes as he thought of the saplings in downtown Newark that never grew much thicker than a man's forearm.

He stopped at the post office to mail the postcards he had written on the road and noticed a 1940s' WPA mural in the lobby, depicting laborers bent under sacks or hoisting bushel baskets onto wagons. He passed the bus station, painted like a stagecoach stop on a Western movie set, and stood in front of The Cooperative Zoo. "I'm in cooperative land," he chuckled as he read the handpainted sign. I haven't been here twenty-four hours and already I've learned a new word—*cooperative*. Outside the small restaurant, an unleashed dog drank water from a metal bowl. Well-worn bicycles were lined up in a bike rack near the front entrance.

Jason walked in through the open door and stepped around a hiker's backpack. There couldn't have been more than ten tables and they all were filled. Jason had to squeeze between a row of chairs to reach an empty stool next to a ledge that faced the street.

But he wasn't interested in the street. He was interested in his coffee. He turned and stood with his back to the window and glanced around the restaurant. A man with a sun tattoo and a velvet top hat set two plates of pancakes erupting with fresh fruit on a table near him. "Of course it's real butter and real maple syrup," Jason heard him say. The customers and workers were indistinguishable from each other, except for the white cotton aprons the workers wore folded and tied around their waists.

Jason understood freaks. He supposed he was one. He'd been called one. Either that or *hippie*. But he was no hippie. He wasn't one of those stoned-out layabouts burning patchouli incense and drinking chamomile tea with his Earth Mama. But these people were not your typical hippies—they were beyond hippie. They looked like they had

Accidental Destination

just stepped out of some backwoods commune. They were prototypical.

A table opened up and Jason grabbed it. He sat down and noticed that at one time it had been a big spool for telephone cable, and was now painted a dull green and brushed over with some sort of clear, thick protective coating. He waited to be offered a glass of water and handed a menu. After several minutes of not being greeted in any way, he stood up, grabbed a menu and coffee cup from a table near the wall and poured himself what was labeled a *bottomless* cup of coffee as he tried unsuccessfully to imagine a cup without a bottom. If it were *truly* bottomless, the coffee wouldn't reach the top—if it stayed in the cup at all. *And what's this—I gotta get my own coffee?*

He sat back down and took a sip of the strongest coffee he'd had in days. This is not bad at all, he thought, as he read the "We Own Our Own Zoo" information section on the back of the menu. He stared at the word *wymyn*, moving his lips as he sounded it out. *Wy-myn*. He learned that in addition to the waitress being a *co-owner*, she was also not a wait*ress*, but a wait*person*.

Where the hell am I? he asked himself. He glanced at the blackboard where the daily specials were written in colored chalk and settled on the huevos rancheros. I'd better go up there and order or I'll die of hunger, he thought. He walked to the counter, passing a sign reading: "This is a Hate-Free Zone." *Damn hippies*, Jason thought, imitating the gruff disapproving tone of former President Nixon and shaking his head so that Tricky Dick's imaginary jowls shook and his own shoulder-length hair fell in front of his eyes.

The wait-whatevershewas who brought his plate was layered in scarves and beaded necklaces. The string of small bells tied around her left ankle jingled when she walked on buffalo sandals. "First time here? You'll like these. The soy burgers are great too, but they won't be ready until lunch. We're always sprouting a fresh batch."

"Thanks. These look good."

And indeed they did. Two corn tortillas slathered with refried beans, then a layer of . . . *alfalfa sprouts?* topped with two sunnyside-up eggs, all doused with a green chili sauce. *Alfalfa sprouts*. Jason couldn't get over it. He had never had huevos rancheros before, but he was fairly certain that they didn't come with sprouts. He cut through the eggs, causing the yolks to run, and scooped up a forkful. They should call these huevos *sprouteros*, he thought.

He noticed a grey plastic bin filled with dirty dishes and cups. I bet they expect me to bus my own dishes too, he thought. He picked up his check. *Hey—they forgot to add the tax! All right!*

As Jason was trying to figure out what kind of tip—if any—was required, he thought about his need to generate some income. He was almost broke and had no idea what kind of work to look for or even how to go about looking for it. At least I have a roof over my head for another month, he thought. I also have to figure out how I'm gonna eat. But even so—I'd rather go hungry and live on the edge here where there's an ocean of possibilities, than to have a full belly and an aching head, stuck in some high-rise, making monthly payments on a revolving nightmare.

In New Jersey, he had landed a gig with an insurance conglomerate as a customer service representative almost by chance. He had walked around Newark one afternoon, applying anywhere that would accept applications, and this company had hired him to *diversify the workforce*—that is, to hire more men for traditionally female jobs. He spent eight hours a day for the next two years in a room with some thirty other reps, most of them women in a wide range of ages and shapes, mostly married or divorced, with kids or grandkids, mortgages and leases, not going anywhere and happy to be right where they were.

He lasted two years—exactly the amount of time the company figured it needed to keep an employee in order to get their money's worth out of the six-week training session—and was let go because—Jason wasn't sure what term they had used—but he had been surprised that both he and the company had hung on so long. He had never made any attempt to hide his disdain for the corporate world. His co-workers said he was too young to appreciate the job security or the good money he was making. "Jason, what are you doing here?" they would sometimes ask after he made a joke at the company's expense or when he told them he was getting ready to play a gig at a local bar.

On weekends, one of Jason's coworkers played accordion in a wedding band. Their conversations about music usually ended the same way: "You can call them schlocky pop standards if you want—but I call them good, steady money," the coworker would say with a shrug of his shoulders. "You'll see, when you've got more than your own mouth to feed." Even the musicians here are lame, Jason thought, as he'd walk away from the discussion singing the chorus to "Time in a Bottle" and gesturing like a lounge singer.

But you have to hand it to these guys, he'd think, how they can complacently suck on The Corporate Tit for thirty-five years, waiting for their pensions to kick in . . . But that'd put me at fifty-four. No way. I'll be as good as dead by then if I stay here like them—regurgitating flow-chart scripts, buying into the contests, drinking my lunches, living for the weekends.

One day the union rep, an affable black man who always had a smile and a handshake for everyone, pulled Jason aside and asked him how he was doing.

"I'm tired of all this bullshit."

"I know you are. So am I—but you always need to say you're doing fine. Whenever anyone asks, just say you're fine."

That's good advice, Jason thought. It works for him. He's a lifer who's been getting over on The Man since day one, but that's not me. It's bad enough to be working here—I'm not gonna kiss their asses too.

It had been a long, drawn-out process, but the first warning led inexorably to the final warning and notice of an appeals process and eventually Jason was out.

A couple of months later, he was walking down the street in Newark and, oblivious, almost walked past the rep. But the rep saw Jason. Again with the smile and the handshake. The first words out of his mouth were: "Hey, Jason—you apply for unemployment yet?" Jason shook his head *no*.

It had never occurred to him. "Well, you should. Time is running out. Take it easy, man." And as quickly as he had appeared, he was gone.

Jason took the last sip of his coffee and remembered a former English teacher who, during the course of a class, had casually mentioned that some people intentionally lose their jobs, collect unemployment insurance and use the time to paint their masterpieces.

He stared at the bottom of his coffee mug. The lyrics "Oh to be back in the land of Coca-Cola" wafted from the speakers attached to the ceiling. Jason correctly surmised that he wouldn't be able to get a Coke or any other carbonated beverage here. Maybe I *should* sign up for unemployment, he thought. But today's Saturday. I'll take care of it first thing Monday morning. Today, I'm gonna check out this little town.

It was impossible for Jason to miss the Saturday Market, sprawling atop two square city blocks, complete with a makeshift performance stage and a separate area for food vendors. The products themselves were craftsy. Jason rolled the word around on his tongue. *Craftsy.* In fact, whatever was sold here had to be handmade or grown, in the case of produce, by the sellers themselves. So, although it resembled a typical street fair, there were no polyester pirate flags, no factory-stamped model cars, military surplus coats, gas masks or plastic geegaws of any kind.

Instead, a woman sold wind chimes fashioned from bent spoons tied together with fishing line and embellished with glass beads, calling them *fairy baths*. The aisles were awash with hand-thrown ceramic cups and plates, beaded jewelry, Myrtlewood boxes and polished stones. One vendor offered concrete mushrooms and peace-sign stepping stones for the garden.

A man who called himself Toad wore oversized swimming goggles and a hand-painted Day-Glo World War I helmet and sold small collections of poems he had stapled together. He had stacks of the booklets—all different sizes and colors—all crinkled and grimy from sitting who knows how long in the child's wagon he pulled behind him. He offered them for a pittance and if anyone bought one, he'd croak: "You want Toad to sign it? You want Toad to sign it?"

I guess they make enough to make it worth their while, Jason thought, so ya gotta give 'em credit. He stopped at a card table piled high with tie-dyed T-shirts. He bought one that read *Member of the University Bong Team* and featured the school mascot clutching a bong and coughing uncontrollably. What's the use of saving my last couple of bucks, he thought. This is priceless.

Near the outer edge of the fair area where there was not much of a crowd, a thin woman stood, eyes half-closed, lips pursed, coaxing a lilting melody from a wooden flute. Jason saw her before he heard the notes, which she blew faintly with perfect intonation. She balanced the flute exactly parallel to the ground and appeared unconcerned whether passersby noticed her or not. She could have been taken for one of the busking musicians, except for the table in front of her that held some forty bamboo flutes of different lengths and diameters. A small handpainted sign read "Jenny's Bamboo Flutes." She wore closely cropped blonde hair and rimless glasses. Her dress, a violet batik design, looked one-of-a-kind, but not craftsy. Everything about her appearance and attitude was understated, as if she were trying not to draw attention to herself.

Jason stood transfixed. When she finished the tune and lowered her flute, he gasped a single syllable: "Hey."

"Hey, yourself."

He looked down at the flutes. "Did you make all these yourself?"

"I even cut and dried the bamboo myself."

Jason looked up from the table. "Cool."

She smiled.

"I've never seen anything like these," he said. "I'll have to pick one up someday. Are you here every week?"

"I have been. But don't wait too long. You never know how long I'll be around. I can even personalize one for you. Carve your totem on it."

"My *totem*?"

"You know—your own personal symbol—your emblem. Mine's a dolphin. Here—see, I carved one on this flute."

Jason squinted at the stylized water mammal. There were even splashes depicting the dolphin rising from the ocean.

"Beautiful . . . beautiful," he mumbled. This girl can talk up a storm and I can't even put a sentence together, he thought. I must be coming off like a freakin' idiot.

"Hi, I'm Jenny," she said. "You look like you might be a jaguar. Think about what you'd like. You'll know."

"Jason," he said, extending his hand. She took it and moved it up and down in a professional, businesslike motion, all the while smiling. "Nice to meet you—Jason."

Was she making fun of him? He didn't know. But she seemed to be enjoying herself. "OK, Jenny. Jenny. I'll be back. I think I need something to eat."

"Try the burgers at Soy Joy. They're not half bad."

"That sounds good. You sounded good. Maybe I will."

He almost stumbled into one of the food tents. She thinks I'm a . . . *jaguar*?

Later, as Jason was walking back to the Anthill, he saw the same cherry tree that had caught his eye on the trip downtown. The branches dripped with ripe, deep red cherries. Many more lay on the grass. These wouldn't last five minutes back in Jersey, he thought. The tree was close enough to the sidewalk that he felt he could get away with picking what he wanted, but he saw someone sitting on the porch of the house.

"Hey—how ya doin'?" Jason yelled in the direction of the man. "Mind if I pick some of these cherries? I'll give you some."

The man half smiled, then shrugged. "No, young man . . . just go ahead and pick as many as you'd like for yourself. I've got plenty already. Do you need a bag? Hold on a minute—I'll get you one."

Well, Jason thought, whatever else happens here, I won't go hungry.

3

THE UNEMPLOYMENT OFFICE SHUFFLE

Monday morning arrived and Jason pulled the thick plate-glass door of the unemployment office open. The smell—a mixture of grime, dampness, stale air and body odor—hit him immediately, like being pounced on by a wet dog. The place was already packed. People stood, waiting in line at any one of five windows, not making eye contact, staring past each other at the walls and floor. Others stood to the side, leafing through pages of job listings or sat, filling out forms with dull, chewed-up pencil stubs. Jason had never seen so many thick beards, steel-toed boots, canvas pants and suspenders in one place.

"I'm glad the cannery laid me off," Jason heard a woman with grey hair past her shoulders say. "I couldn't take another day sweating in those hip boots, squirting away carrot peelings with that high-pressure hose."

"Yeah," the guy standing next to her said. "And because they won't say for sure that they'll hire us back, we have to go through this whole song-and-dance routine, even though everyone knows full well we're going back to work when the fall harvest comes in."

"It's a good scam for the company and we get a paid vacation out of it. No complaints here."

Jason picked up a brochure titled *Benefit Information: Frequently Asked Questions* and began reading as he fell into the shortest line.

It says here this is the *employment* office, but I wonder how many people actually find employment here, he thought. Jason knew that the nickname *unemployment office* came from the checks received from unemployment insurance, a system designed to help those who—through no fault of their own—had lost their jobs get through a rough patch while they are actively seeking employment. Those were the exact words on the brochure—*through no fault of their own* and *actively seeking employment*.

Neither of these phrases fit Jason's situation. His old job had been hanging by a thread for months. There was no room for doubt when his supervisor checked the *Job in Jeopardy* box in Jason's personnel folder during his last performance review. She had even asked him to initial it. It was the final phase in the firing countdown. While any one of his transgressions may not have been a firing offense, Jason knew that he'd been turning in a generally lackluster performance while not kissing ass or fitting the corporate mold. The final straw came when he stopped showing up regularly for work, thinking he'd use up his paid sick leave before the ax fell.

I need to come up with a good story, he thought as he noticed the stands for the American and state flags were pitted and covered with dust, and the concrete floor, with its naturally rough surface of small imbedded stones, had soaked up so much mud, grime and coffee over the years that cleaning it would be a major undertaking, if it could be done at all. With all these people looking for work, I wonder why no one's hired a decent janitor for this place, he asked himself.

Look at all these people. They've got experience doing things I can't even imagine. Why would anyone want to hire me? The only real job I ever had, I can't even use as a reference. If something doesn't turn up quick, or I can't collect unemployment, I'll have to hitchhike back to New Jersey at the end of the month.

Accidental Destination

Jason made his way to the head of the line, and the employee who handed him the application reminded him of any number of his former co-workers: compliant cogs following a script. He knew that all he had to do was put the right answers in the right blanks and the money would be his. The form was easy enough to navigate until he got to the space marked *Reason for Leaving*. He knew that if he said he had quit his job, he would be ineligible for benefits. He hadn't *quit . . . technically*, but . . . I'll put down *illness*, he thought. It's true—I was sick of my fucking job. If they question me, I'll just say I got sick and they cut me loose for missing too many days.

Jason handed the clerk the completed form and was told they would contact his former employer and that he needed to return in two weeks for an interview.

Two weeks later he was back, seated in one of the rows of orange, hard plastic chairs riveted to the concrete, staring through tinted windows that made the world outside seem as bleak as the waiting area inside. When his name was called, he stood up, and the interviewer escorted him through a maze of grey metal desks, some with framed family photos on top, others with small jars filled with candies. Accounting for differences in the types of business, Jason found this setup wasn't much different from his old corporate job. Worker bees are worker bees everywhere, he thought. Not even the hives change much.

"Have a seat, please," his interviewer said, motioning toward a mismatched metal chair next to her desk. She sat down, picked up a pen and said, "I'll get right to the point—your company never challenges their claims. They just pay out." She tapped her finger on Jason's form. "But I see here you left your last job because of . . . *illness?*"

"Well . . ." Jason said—*Here it comes*, he thought—"I fell ill for a while and they wouldn't keep me. It wasn't my fault at all."

"Whatever the case, we need to know that you're capable of working now."

"Of course I am. Just look at me."

"You need to be *certified*. You need to bring us a doctor's certificate that states you're able to work."

"OK. If that's what I need to do. I can do that."

Jason knew enough not to argue the point. He was in good physical shape and had no trouble finding a doctor to give him a clean bill of health.

Checks began appearing in his post office box each Friday morning, as regular as if an employer had handed them to him personally. The first time he pulled an envelope out, he slapped it against his hand, looked up at the mural with the farmworker bent under a sack of crops she was picking, and wiggled his toes. This is good for a whole six months and all I have to do is mail in a form every couple of weeks and maybe submit to an interview every now and then, he thought. For that I'm making almost as much as I did at Conglomerated Insurance. When my unemployment runs out, I can always apply for food stamps and maybe snag a few bucks as a pick-up laborer. Tim told me Emerald is an easy place to get by in—you just have to know the ins and outs—and the folks around here aren't shy about sharing their know-how.

The sunlight hit Jason full in the face as he walked out of the post office to find a place to cash his check. He saw a man, who called himself North Jetty Bill, standing on the sidewalk with a guitar slung over his shoulder, selling cassettes and playing for tips. He was missing a front tooth and had a harmonica holder wrapped around his neck.

I like this guy, Jason thought. He's not begging. He's got a little business going. Ya gotta give him credit. Jason waited until the man finished his song, emptied his pockets and said, "Hey man, I dig what you're doing. Here's all the money I got on me."

North Jetty Bill handed him a cassette and said, "Thanks, bro. And here—each cassette you buy entitles you to a free sticker. The sticker was printed with Bill's name, telephone number and the phrase: Embracing the World One Song at a Time.

When Jason got back to the Anthill, his fingers were itching to make some music. He found Tim changing his guitar strings. "It took you long enough to get that first check," Tim said as he slid a string into its tuning peg. "Next time just say you were laid off. *Always* say you were laid off—usually they just pay out without challenging it. Don't make it harder on yourself than it has to be."

"Yeah. All I'm doing is interpreting a grey area in my favor. I'm not breaking any laws—and even if I am—they're not gonna come after me for a few lousy bucks. It's not like I'm hurting anyone."

I can see how people make a lifestyle out of scamming, Jason thought. This definitely has merit. Besides, Uncle Sam has spent enough of my tax money in Vietnam. He can afford to subsidize his nephew here at home for a while.

4

CLEVELAND SLIM & THE STONED GALORE SLACKERS

Days and weeks passed. Most mornings, Jason sat in his room reading books or trying to coax a new song from his guitar. He didn't know anyone outside of the Anthill, and Tim was the only one there he hung with. He knew no one would come knocking on his door, but he sometimes wished someone would. He had no one to call within 3,000 miles and no phone to call them with. Nothing much was happening. No one was going anywhere and there wasn't anywhere to go.

He flipped through the spiral notebook of songs and poems he had brought with him, making changes in pencil. He bought a portable typewriter and tapped out the haiku he had scribbled in his pocket notebook on his trip to Emerald, blending images of the road's stainless steel truckstops and boarded-up service stations with nature's fluid prairies and sleepy mountain peaks.

When he could sit still no longer, usually by 10 a.m., Jason went out and explored the town. He often headed to the library, playing records in the listening room or flipping through the stacks in the poetry section, trying to discover a poet on his own, one he had never heard of, one no one had recommended to him. There, a tarot card zodiac-like drawing on a book cover caught his eye. Galway Kinnell: *The Book of Nightmares*. He read a few lines, then closed the book. This might be good stuff, he thought, but it's like reading through molasses. He grabbed another. Ted Hughes: *The Crow*. He's supposed to be good, Jason thought, but I don't get this guy either. He slid the book back and pulled out another. Lew Welch: *Hermit Poems*. This guy is straightforward and tells it plain, Jason thought. He sat in the aisle on a stepstool and read the slim volume all the way through.

He had no local ID, so he couldn't get a library card to check out any books. He glanced at the inside cover and noticed that no one had checked it out yet. I'd like to slip out of here with this one, he thought, but this book is too good to steal. Maybe someone else will discover it like I did. He slid it back into exactly the same spot he had removed it from.

Lew Welch makes it seem so easy, just a matter of observing what is and representing it with a single image, he thought. Like Leonard Cohen's "Bird on a Wire." How many birds on wires have I seen in my lifetime? And I never wrote a song about any of them.

Jason walked up and down the railroad tracks. He ate avocado sandwiches. He bought an old bicycle. He typed up a new poem here and there, trying different designs on the page.

One evening, he sat in the Rose Garden, attempting to capture the shimmering colors of the rain, trying to come up with a poem that could match the fragrance of a cluster of roses harmonizing with the flow of the river in the background, moving words around the page like rose petals cascading to the ground.

Roses are a tired cliché, Jason knew, but there are so many species, so many states of unfoldment, so many colors, so many fragrances. But it was the rain that transformed them, the droplets clinging to the petals, each drop a prismatic world, their combined weight easing the petals to the ground one by one, nestling them in a transitory bed for whatever dreams lay beneath these thorny, fragrant universal symbols of love.

I could bring Flute Girl here, he thought. Even if she would agree to go out with me, I don't want to bring her to my sad excuse for a crashpad—but I could bring her here. Drizzling rain would enfold us in the moonlight, we'd cling to each other like raindrops on rose petals and lay together, one, in each other's arms . . . Yes, I could definitely bring her here. I *will* definitely bring her here.

This particular morning began like every other morning, with a trip to the kitchen to make himself his morning coffee. A big black man with grey curly hair and a big belly sat at the table strumming a cheap acoustic guitar. He had to have been at least forty. "Hi, I'm Cleveland Slim," he said, half getting up, extending his right hand to Jason. "They calls me that 'cause I'm from Cleveland. I'm here and then I'm gone. Boom." His fingers felt like sausages.

"What's doen?" Jason replied, holding his empty coffee cup, listening as Slim half whispered, half sang: "Ain't no one wan' t hear da blues. Blues ain't good fo' nufin'—Ain't no goood fo' nufin' a-tall . . ." He strummed a chord here and there, banging on the floor, keeping time with his left foot. He seemed to be making up the words and rhythm as he went along, as if he were thinking out loud, trying to figure his own story out. Jason ran his fingers through his hair and Slim stopped playing. "But they's all I know," he said. "All I can do."

Jason recognized Slim from Big Papa's Downhome Skillet, a coffeehouse with a makeshift stage and killer homefries, where musicians could score acoustic gigs for tips. Slim performed there most Friday mornings. Jason asked him what he was doing *here*. In *this* kitchen.

"I'm waiting on a place of my own." Slim rested his arms on the guitar. "Jus' here till then. This place is an anthill, I know, but we all do what we gotta t su'vive."

Jason said nothing about playing guitar himself. He gawked at how genuinely Slim embodied the blues—sitting in this dark kitchen, unshaven, jobless, precariously close to homeless, waiting for who knows what, while effortlessly fretting a chord with a single finger of his left hand and conjuring unexpected harmonies with his fingerpicking.

This guy's the real thing, Jason thought. Now that I'm here with Slim, I can ask him anything I want. But Slim didn't wait for a question. "See, ya gotta have a song. A song ya can play any time. If ya ain't got that, ya ain't got no right to call yo'sef a musician. It don't matter none how ya play it. Take 'In the Midnight Hour.'" He strummed a Bb chord. "See now, ya can sing it real slow—like this . . . "Ahmmm . . . gon . . . na . . . waaait . . . till . . . the . . . miid . . . niight . . . ow . . . ur . . . See, or ya can sing it fast . . ." Slim kept repeating the line, running the words together until their meaning fluctuated with each shift of his phrasing or tempo.

And he did it in *Bb*. B *flat!* This guy doesn't even play in regular keys, Jason thought, moving his head back and forth in time to the music. How Slim came up with this stuff, Jason had no idea. He also had no idea why Slim was telling him all this.

Tim walked into the kitchen and immediately raised his right hand for a high five. "Heeey, Slim, man, Good to see you—Gimme some skin."

"Hey—Tim brotherman," Slim replied, slapping his hand hard. "Where ya been keepin' yo'sef? Thanks fer lettin' me crash here on the down low fer a few days."

"Glad to do it, man."

Tim *knew Slim—and*—Slim didn't even have a place to call his own? What a mind-blowing upside-down world.

Jason was more in Tim's league. Tim was from Florida and spent almost every morning shut up in his room making up songs. He'd sit in there with his guitar and notebook and see what he could come up with. But he was in no hurry to perform on stage. For him that wasn't the goal. He played for gatherings of friends, for fun. He always had his guitar with him and he loved to make songs up.

"You mean you *write* your own songs?" Jason had asked the first time he heard Tim use that phrase.

"No, ma'n. I *make them up*," he had replied, slipping into a slight Southern drawl. "You gotta have yer own tunes or it du'ent mean shit. You ain't nothin' but a cover band without 'em. That's what Ronnie sa'id."

Tim claimed he had been a roadie for Lynyrd Skynyrd, and that he had hung out with them at a place called The Jug in Jacksonville. He certainly had plenty of stories, es-

Accidental Destination

pecially when he got to sucking on a bottle of Jack Daniels. "And being on the road ain't no good life. We was at this roadhouse one morning and I complained my eggs was cold. Ronnie said, 'Shut up an' eat 'em.' Just like that. He said, 'Shut up an' eat 'em.' And it's not just the food—it's the long bus rides and the venue owners always trying to short you. That's why they all got so rowdy. Ronnie was a Golden Gloves, but he'd get sloppy drunk and start fights he couldn't win, being as he was so wasted. One night he got whupped so bad, someone wrote 'Lynyrd Got Skynyrd' in lipstick on the side of his bus."

Jason began hanging out with Tim and his friend Marshall. Most afternoons Tim would head over to Marshall's and Jason would go with him. Marshall had his own house and a full-time job, two things that made him unique among the people Jason knew. Marshall was a few years older than Jason, installed telephones for a living, wore a full beard and was able to effortlessly figure out songs from the record. As he listened and played along, he'd retune his guitar if it was a bit sharp or flat. He'd say things like, "This one's in E, but it sounds like he's using a capo and playing a C chord. You might as well play it the same way they do." But Marshall, even more than Tim, who claimed he was just waiting until he made up enough good songs, had no desire whatsoever to play music outside of his home. "It's not my thing," he'd say. "I've got too much other stuff going on." Tim and Marshall could burn it up, but they didn't care. Music for them was nothing more than a way to pass the lazy rain-filled days and evenings when they had nothing better to do, which was more often than not.

The jam sessions invariably began with a bowl of weed as soon as Marshall came home from work. Tim had a key to the house and was usually a few beers to the good by this time. They smoked nonchalantly, as if pot were legal and it was no different than unwinding with a couple of beers after work. In New Jersey, Jason and his friends would always ask, "Is he cool?" This meant would he get freaked out or narc on us if he knows we smoke pot? Here, it seemed, everyone was cool.

"Oregon recently decriminalized marijuana," Marshall said, as he used the scissors on his Swiss Army knife to trim the bud he had just slid off a Thai stick. "Now, if you get caught with less than an ounce, it's just a fine, like a parking ticket—not even a misdemeanor."

"In Jersey you can still go to jail for it," Jason replied.

Marshall rolled a joint, put it in his mouth, and pulled it out slowly, twisting it to make sure the gumless paper held tight. "Probably the worst thing here is that they confiscate your weed." He held the unlit joint between his index and middle fingers. "And you know, I bet no one's smoking any more here than where they lock you up for it. If you're going to smoke, you're going to smoke. If not, this isn't going to get you started."

"You always have really good pot," Jason said.

"I buy it like I buy my groceries. It's always on my shopping list," Marshall replied.

"Would you hurry up and light that thing already?" Tim asked. "It's not even lit and you're already bogarting it."

At first, Jason enjoyed jamming with Tim and Marshall, but soon he felt as if his days were trapped in a repeating loop. The same old songs, the same old riffs, the same old living room, the same old, same old.

All three played acoustic guitars. Jason augmented his friends' rhythm chords with lead guitar. But he wasn't singing, he wasn't playing any of the songs that *he* had made up, he wasn't making progress on his own thing.

I suppose it's my own fault, Jason thought, as he lit a match to take another toke from a small onyx pipe. I get too fuckin' wasted to introduce my own songs. Not that they would listen to them anyway. And if I have to hear Marshall croon Fleetwood Mac's "Landslide" one more time with that earnest expression on his face, I might lose it. There isn't enough beer or smoke in the world to make that go down any easier.

Maybe I should get an electric guitar or learn to play bass or something. Everyone here in Emerald has an acoustic guitar or some kind of acoustic instrument—

Accidental Destination

there's We Lasses, that all-girl Irish group who cram themselves into a corner at The Zoo every Friday night, that bluegrass band that plays the Public Market on Sunday afternoons, and there's fiddlers, dulcimer players, and guitarists with harmonica racks up the ying yang strumming cowboy chords like they're going out of style. There's even stiff competition to play for tips at Big Papa's.

I need a *real* band—playing *real* gigs—*paying* gigs. I dig these guys, but I can't get sucked into their trip.

"I think this is spent," Jason said, as he handed the pipe back to Marshall.

5

ODD JOBS & NEW DIGS

Time passed imperceptibly, unemployment insurance ran out, and Jason needed to find some other way to stay afloat.

Folks at the Anthill sometimes picked up a day or two of work at the University Job Service, a small, cinderblock building near the edge of campus. It was open to the community at large, and, on this particular morning, Jason and fellow Anthill denizen Ginzo snagged a job laying sewage drain pipe for an optometrist who was building himself a house and acting as his own contractor.

Ginzo drove his '68 Rambler to the site, passing a joint to Jason. He took a toke and held it in. As he exhaled he said, "We'd better get rid of this. That guy over there looks like he might be the boss."

"Don't worry about it," Ginzo replied, taking the roach from Jason and stubbing it out in the ashtray. "Look at that dork with his tassel loafers and clipboard. He doesn't have a clue."

Ginzo got out of the car, smiled at the man, and said, "Good morning, sir. We're the temporary workers I believe you are expecting." After brief introductions, the optometrist explained that the ditches had already been dug, and that the eight-foot long, twelve-inch diameter PVC pipes were laid out end to end along the sides. All they had to do, he said, was to drop a pipe into the ditch, fit a rubber seal ring on one end, swab the edge of the pipe next to it with glue and then push them together. He ran through the instructions quickly, as if the procedure was common knowledge. "Just get as much done as you can today. I'm guessing this is probably a two-day job. I'll be back to check on you later." He turned and climbed into his freshly waxed pick-up.

"Look—even the tires are shiny," Ginzo said, as the man drove away.

The sun grew hot, but Jason and Ginzo worked quickly. "He won't be back till late afternoon. If we lay enough pipe, we can kick back and just look busy when we see him coming," Ginzo said.

Ariel Ginsburg had wanted everyone to call him *Ari*, but the moniker *Ginzo* was slapped on him the first day he took a room at the Anthill and it stuck despite his best efforts. Ginzo was an artist who specialized in large three-dimensional paintings that he made by sewing stuffing into canvas pouches and then sewing the pieces together. Life was a work of art in progress for Ginzo.

They had been working on and off for five hours and the pipes were becoming more difficult to lift and push into each other. It was time to kick back. They sat on a pipe at the edge of the trench and fired up a joint in the large lot flanked by Douglas firs. "Although all this will soon be covered with dirt, it still can be a work of art," Ginzo said. He languidly stood up, climbed back into the trench and began painting the end of a pipe with so much pink goo that it looked like flames were shooting out after the two pipes were inserted. Ginzo's brushwork became more and more fanciful with each pipe, and Jason wondered if this might be a problem. "It's just glue," Ginzo said. "The pipes are stuck together good."

At around three, the optometrist returned. "That's good work for today," he said. "I'll see you back here tomorrow morning at seven, OK?" He fished a roll of cash out of his pocket, peeled off a few bills and handed them to Jason and Ginzo. He gestured to a half-empty crate of grapes in the back of his truck. "You boys hungry? You're welcome to them."

Jason and Ginzo sat on the hood of the Rambler and filled

Accidental Destination

their bellies. There were more grapes than they could eat. They ate so many that they each felt as if they had drunk a gallon of grape juice. Jason looked back at the work they had done. "You can't say we didn't lay a lot of pipe today," he said.

"Yeah. But there's still a lot left to do," Ginzo replied.

The next morning, the optometrist was waiting by the trench. When Jason and Ginzo got out of the car, his hands began to shake. "I'm sorry, but I can't use you boys anymore," he said. "The inspector came by yesterday afternoon and said all this pipe needs to be pulled out and redone."

"How come?" Jason asked.

"All that glue. It can't be sticking out like that."

"What?" Ginzo replied. "You didn't say anything about neatness. They're stuck together real good."

"Maybe. But it didn't pass inspection."

Jason was not surprised. The optometrist looked at the ditch, and Jason figured he was calculating the cost of new materials and union labor as he shook his head and mumbled, "I guess you get what you pay for."

Driving back to town, Ginzo said, "That's what he gets for trying to go cheap. He didn't know what he was doing."

Another time, Jason worked for a week at a furniture warehouse, the longest he had ever held one of these pick-up jobs. The work was simple: unpacking furniture—dressers, end tables, chairs, dining tables and the like—from their cardboard shipping boxes and the plastic they were wrapped in. He worked eight hours a day, with a half hour off for lunch and two fifteen-minute breaks. Of all his minimum-wage gigs, Jason liked this warehouse job the best. He enjoyed sitting in the breakroom—really no more than a small area off the loading dock with a few benches—and watching the clock with the full-time employees with their dented metal lunchboxes, thermoses and bologna-and-cheese sandwiches.

Enjoying the warm air blowing in through the loading dock door, Jason pulled a package of peanut butter crackers from the vending machine and wondered what it would be like to punch a time clock here every day. I could do this, he thought. No more standing in line, begging for temp jobs—no more uncertainty, no more counting pennies, no more hand-to-mouth existence. He pulled a guitar pick out of his pocket and twirled it between his thumb and forefinger.

One of the drivers called to him: "Hey, Jason—break's over—hop in the truck. The boss wants you to help me make the deliveries today. Our regular guy's out."

"Sure," Jason replied, slipping the pick back into his pocket and climbing into the truck. "That's cool."

"The people we deliver to are super picky," were the first words out of Jerry's mouth as he drove out of the industrial park. "Make sure you don't bump any of their new furniture or ding their paint or there'll be hell to pay. The folks who buy this crap make a stink over every little thing."

Jason wouldn't bump any furniture or ding any paint. He could hardly believe he was being driven around in a big delivery truck, stopping every now and then to off-load (he was already picking up the lingo) a dining room set or some other furniture grouping and that he was getting paid to do it. I could *definitely* do this, Jason thought, getting into the groove after several deliveries, the passenger side window rolled down, the radio blasting "Fortunate Son" by Creedence Clearwater Revival.

"If you don't mind, I have to stop off at my place for a minute," Jerry said. "It's not too far out of the way. I just need to pick up the shopping list my wife left for me this morning. She'll kill me if I forget anything on it." Without waiting for a reply, he swung off the main road, made a couple of left turns and drove down a street that was much different from the ones they had been delivering furniture to. The bushes were untrimmed, the aluminum storm doors were missing screens, bicycles and wagons were scattered in the yards, and a couple of houses had those moveable basketball hoops in the middle of their driveways.

This place is *unkempt*, Jason thought. Although he lived in a much funkier area, something about this street made his toes curl. He sensed it was a neighborhood of families

Accidental Destination

barely scraping by, sacrificing to put baseball mitts on their kids' hands and disposable diapers on their babies' butts. This was not a situation Jason wanted to be in, even in his imagination. I might be poor, but at least I'm not tied down to anyone, he thought. No woman's ever gonna put a rope around *my* neck.

The truck stopped in a cul-de-sac. Jerry hopped out and walked quickly up the path to his house. "Come on," he said, stepping through the front door and motioning for Jason to follow. "I'll just be a second."

Jason looked around the living room. It was filled with furniture. New furniture. More furniture than a room should hold. And then there were the decorative touches, such as the pinkish-purple curtains hanging on fluted metal rods and the stained-glass ornaments dangling from the center of each window. Jason raised an eyebrow.

"My wife," Jerry said. "She calls them window *treatments*. She makes me buy all this stuff. Just because I get a discount on it, she thinks she can go overboard." Jason couldn't imagine having this much furniture in so small a space, no matter how little it cost. More to the point, he couldn't imagine himself living in a house decorated like this. A ceramic goose dressed in a hand-sewn smock greeted visitors at the door. The cacophony of colors and fabrics— the geese on the wallpaper borders—it was all so . . .

"I'm not crazy about it myself," Jerry said, "but I love her."

Jason shook his head up and down absentmindedly.

When they arrived back at the warehouse, the loading dock was deserted. Jerry pulled the truck's back door open and sat down, dangling his feet off the edge of the truck. "Take a load off. We've got another fifteen minutes before quitting time," he said.

"You mean we're just gonna sit here?"

"If you want, you can sweep out the back of the truck or fold up the furniture pads," he said. "But there's no reason you have to stick around. We're all done for the day. I can't punch out till five, but I can punch you out if you want. Right now, I'm gonna kick back for fifteen minutes on the boss's dime. You did good today."

"Thanks." Jason shrugged. What else could he say or do? That you're not getting over on The Man to the tune of fifteen minutes—he's getting over on you, making you wait, showing you who's boss? Or that I wouldn't be in any hurry to go home either if I lived in a house like yours?

Jason liked and even admired this warehouseman—just another one of the shitjob laborers of the world with similar stories, different dialects and blind faith that elbow grease and sticktoitiveness would inevitably lead them to their slice of The American Dream. But this was not Jason's path, either now or in any future he could foresee. I hope this guy has a Plan B, Jason thought, but who knows? Maybe this floats his boat.

Jason worked in other warehouses, hauled dirt in wheelbarrows, moved filing cabinets for a law office—anything where someone needed temporary hourly muscle. One day, Jason, and two others he didn't know, landed a job loading a U-Haul truck for a college professor who was moving to South Carolina. Jason bicycled twenty or so blocks north of the university to an area he had never been in before. The Saturday sun was burning away the morning chill. He took a deep breath and wiggled his toes. He couldn't say exactly what made the neighborhood so inviting. These weren't cookie-cutter mansions like the dream house of the optometrist he had laid pipe for, nor were they like the run-down single-family houses where he lived. These houses were spaced further apart than in Jason's neighborhood, the lawns were all mown—manicured, really—the shrubs were trimmed and flowers were planted in discernable patterns. Annuals hung in baskets on the porches.

Jason rode his bike up the driveway of the house with the U-Haul parked in front, and the woman standing on the porch asked, "Are you here to help us move?" Jason nodded. "Talk to my husband—he's over there." She pointed to the truck and yelled. "Hey, Glenn—this young man is here to help us load up."

The man finished loading a box and stepped out of the

Accidental Destination

truck, his hand extended. "I'm Glenn and I'm glad you're here. We've got to load up this whole truck with furniture today. Monday I'm driving it down to Clemson—C'mon." Jason followed Glenn to the second floor, noticing the walnut-stained stairs and baseboards. "This is a really nice house," he said.

"Yes. It is. But we're leaving it. On to bigger and better things, I suppose." He spoke in measured tones. How much better could South Carolina be than this? Jason wondered, as Glenn tipped a dresser toward him. "Let's move this one down first," he said.

Jason looked out a window and saw a large cypress tree, its leaves nearly brushing the house. *Nice*, he thought. The dresser was also nice. Not that showroom-fresh, faux-distressed veneer (Jason was also becoming knowledgeable about furniture) he was used to unboxing. This was more . . . *substantial*. Jason and the others, whose names he never did catch, spent the next three hours loading furniture and boxes with Glenn, who directed the operation, not in a bossy way, but as if he really appreciated the help, all while working as hard as any of them.

"It's time to eat," a voice called, as Glenn's wife motioned them all to an oak table with eight carved wooden chairs in the only room that not much progress had been made on. The table was crammed with cold cuts, sliced cheeses, an assortment of breads and rolls, and cans of soda. "I'm sorry, all we have are paper plates. The dishes have already been packed away," she said. "And if any of you doesn't eat meat, you can see we've got cheese and tomatoes and sprouts . . ."

Jason had never been fed on a job before, and he certainly didn't eat this well in his own house. In fact, he was getting tired of fried potatoes and cold cereal. His stomach rumbled as he eyed the spread set before him. He hadn't had cold cuts—fresh, deli cold cuts, not the stuff from those little plastic packages—since he left New Jersey.

"You can thank my wife Gina for all this," Glenn said as they all sat down to eat.

As Jason grabbed a slice of pumpernickel, a girl about his age walked past the table and waved in Gina and

Glenn's direction. "See ya," she said to no one in particular. She couldn't have been here the whole time, Jason thought. I would have noticed her. She wore a maroon sweater with faded jeans, and her long, chestnut hair fell across her face so that only one eye was visible. Athletic . . . *totally* out of my league, Jason thought. So *this* is where girls like her come from.

"That's our daughter Jeanette—she's a French major," Gina said, waving a plastic fork in her direction.

She looks pretty high maintenance, Jason thought. And what would she see in me anyway? I'm just some poor fuck-head strumming a guitar in his spare time and I've got nothing but spare time. For that matter, what would Flute Girl see in me? I bet guys hit on her all the time, standing out there in the Saturday Market like that. But even so . . . I should drop by with my guitar and see what happens, see if something unfolds naturally. It beats just exchanging pleasantries every time I get the nerve up to walk past her booth. I couldn't take it if I asked her out and she shut me down. But I can't just not do anything. What is it about that girl that makes me tongue-tied whenever I get close to her?

They ate without hurrying. "Have some more," Gina kept saying before anyone's plate was even close to empty. When no one could eat another bite, it was back to loading the truck.

The afternoon flew by and soon Glenn pulled down the sliding door on the U-Haul. "Anyone care for a beer?" he asked as Gina appeared with four bottles of Miller and passed them around. Jason took a swig. It went down easy. As they were finishing their beers and shaking hands good-bye, Jason had to stop himself from saying, "Thanks for your hospitality."

As he pedaled back to the Anthill with some cash in his pocket, Jason realized he was hungry again. He thought about what he could pick up for dinner. He had worked up a thirst that one beer didn't quench. One of those hot, store-roasted chickens and a couple of quarts of Miller should do it, he thought.

When Jason got home, he found Double Fault, the

Accidental Destination

newest member in the revolving cast of Anthillians, sitting at the kitchen table with a guy she introduced as her long-distance boyfriend from Klamath Falls. She had invited herself into Jason's bed one morning several days ago, saying she had *heard a noise* and *was scared*. She had been wearing pajamas and smiling the whole time. Her hair smelled like burnt toast and she didn't even let him wrap his arms around her. He had never been attracted to the short-haired tennis player, and that didn't change, even as she jumped around restlessly in bed with him. Nothing had happened and when she hopped out of bed several minutes later, she acted as if nothing *had* happened. Jason knew it wouldn't happen again. Like it was a big joke he wasn't in on.

"He's just here for tonight," she said.

That's a long way to travel for some cold fish pussy, Jason thought. Bob Dylan was singing on a portable cassette player. *Tha-row yer tiiiiicket in the wiiiiind . . . Tha-row yer suuootcaaaase out theeere tooo . . .* Jason had never heard anything like it, although he recognized the voice and the song. "Where'd ya get that?" he asked.

"It's a soundboard tape from a Rolling Thunder show. I know a guy," Double Fault's boyfriend said.

Jason cracked open a quart. "You want some, man? The champagne of bottled beers."

Double Fault stood up. "I can't stand this kind of music," she said. "You know where to find me when you're ready." She walked out of the kitchen, leaving Jason and the boyfriend to listen to the rest of the cassette.

"You like this?" the boyfriend asked. "I'll make you a copy and also send a couple of others I know you'll like when I get back home."

Jason and the boyfriend finished the beer. He didn't appear to be in any hurry to join Double Fault in her bedroom.

Later that night, Jason heard laughing protests coming from her room, followed by moans of pleasure and more laughter.

A week later, the cassettes arrived as promised. I meet a lot of interesting people here, Jason thought, but I don't know how much more of this I can stand. This place is nuts and if I stay here much longer, I'm gonna go nuts along with the rest of them.

The days grew colder, work grew scarcer, and Jason kept scraping by. He always managed to scrounge together enough for the rent each month, but it wasn't easy. The other day he had gone out with a group of Anthillians to pick rhubarb at a local farm. They didn't even make minimum wage, but they took home all the rhubarb they could sneak out. Now, one of the residents—Jason still couldn't bring himself to think of them as roommates—had cooked several rhubarb pies with whole wheat crusts and a pan full of tarts as a kind of communal meal. Hungry as he was, he couldn't swallow more than a sliver. Although it would practically clean him out, Jason decided to treat himself to lasagna at the new Italian restaurant downtown. I need some soul food tonight, he thought.

As he sat waiting for his meal at a table covered with a red-and-white plastic checkered tablecloth, he buttered and ate the slices of bread that had been placed in a basket on his table. This isn't Italian bread, he thought. It's just the same spongy air bread they sell at Safeway. It's barely bread at all. I could eat the whole thing and still have room for the lasagna. He took a sip of water from an oversized plastic glass.

When the waiter set the plate of lasagna on the table, Jason stared at the small oval dish. Before he took a bite, he pried the layers apart with his fork and noticed dry white blobs resting on the bright red tomato sauce between them. He knew immediately what they were and called the waiter back over. "Excuse me," he asked. "What are these?"

"What are what?"

"These white blobs."

"Oh, that's *cottage cheese*." The waiter answered sotto voce, as if he were divulging a secret ingredient.

"I've never heard of cottage cheese in lasagna. It's *always* ricotta. It's *gotta* be ricotta."

"Well," the waiter replied, "the cook is Greek."

Accidental Destination

Jason remembered a neighborhood restaurant behind a bar in Elizabeth, New Jersey that was little more than a windowless basement room that had to be accessed through an unmarked side door. The lasagna must have been at least six layers thick, each one of them spread thickly with ricotta and ingredients from an old family recipe that had probably never been written down. It was the only lasagna he had ever tasted that was better than the lasagna his mother had taught him how to make. One night Jason had taken her there. She took a bite and, mozzarella dripping from her fork, said, "This is *very* good." They both were diplomatic enough not to compare it aloud to their own lasagnas.

Ordering lasagna at a restaurant was always a crap-shoot, but Jason had expected at least a reasonable facsimile for his hard-earned rhubarb-cutting money. He stood up, carefully folded his napkin and dropped it on the plate. "Take this slop back to the cook and tell him to feed it to the pigs." He heard his New Jersey accent coming out. Shit, he thought, I sound like a character in *The Godfather*. But I don't think anyone's gonna come after me for not showing respect. You can't even get a slice of pizza in this town.

Jason returned to the Anthill and the residents were still going at the rhubarb full blast. They were passing around a bottle of wine and talking all at once as if they didn't have a care in the world. I *really* gotta get out of this place, Jason thought. Nothing's gonna change for me unless I get outta here.

"That's red wine, I hope," Jason said, holding his hand out for the bottle.

When Tim mentioned that Scratchy had a space available in his attic, Jason was ready to grab it. "Scratchy. That's a weird name," Jason said.

"Yeah—his real name's Pete. You'll see why they call him Scratchy when you meet him. Just make sure you don't call him that to his face. But he's cool. He plays guitar too. He's something else. You'll see."

When Scratchy found out that Jason also played guitar

and had a Brazilian rosewood Martin, he asked him to move in right away. The walls of the attic (the roof of the house, actually) were angled, but it was a large space. Jason slid his foam pad under the exposed 2x4 studs. A couple of folding chairs and a card table were set up near a porthole-sized window. What more do I need? Jason thought, picking up his guitar, sitting down, and peering out the window at two sets of railroad tracks not two blocks away.

6

SCRATCHY &
THE GRANGE HALL GIG

Scratchy carried **his** guitar in a cardboard case, made up train songs and belted out obscure hobo songs from the Great Depression. Even in his living room or kitchen, he played to an imaginary audience. He'd crank out song after song, using the most rudimentary chords on what must have been the cheapest Gibson available and, if the songs weren't his, he'd be scrupulous about naming the authors. He also knew quite a bit about them and couldn't help sharing the information. "That was one by poet and singer Harry McClintock," he'd say. "'Haywire Mac' they called him and with good reason. He was one crazy rail rider."

Scratchy's record crate was loaded with discs by artists Jason had never heard of—Jim Ringer, Kinky Friedman, Utah Phillips, Boxcar Willie . . .

He had also never heard of these record labels—Rounder, Flying Fish, Old Dominion . . . Before he met Scratchy, his idea of folk music had been Crosby, Stills, Nash and Young or Richard and Mimi Fariña.

Jason flipped through the records. There's a whole world of acoustic music out there, he thought, a world that's close to the earth, authentic—a world that Scratchy inhabits and I didn't even know existed.

Scratchy was some ten years older than Jason, and although Jason wasn't impressed with his guitar playing or singing, he was blown away by his songs, his tales of travel and making do, but most of all, by the fact that he was out there performing to anyone who would listen. Jason didn't call Pete "Scratchy" to his face. No one did. But when he thought you weren't looking, he'd scratch his arms and legs lightly and twist his upper lip back and forth. His full mustache made the lip twitch seem somehow natural, nothing more than a quirky mannerism.

Jason had noticed that Scratchy didn't work—not even a scam every now and then. "Hey man," Jason asked one day when his curiosity got the better of him, "You're always playing your guitar or working on a song or something involving music. How come you don't have to work?"

"I get money from the government," Scratchy replied, pouring ketchup on his freshly boiled noodles. He said it in a way that didn't encourage further conversation. "Disability from when I was in the Navy," he added.

"Don't get me wrong. I think it's great, but you're not fucked up. You don't *seem* fucked up—not like most thirty-whatever-year-olds."

Scratchy stared at Jason, crinkled his brow, and took a long look into Jason's eyes, his fingers resting lightly on his legs. "What do you mean?" he asked in measured tones.

Now Jason wanted to scratch himself. "It's just that you're not like most people your age—You're cool—You're doing your thing—You're not living the straight life like most people are."

"Well . . . thanks." Scratchy scooped up a tablespoon of elbow macaroni. "Hey listen, Jason—want to accompany me tomorrow night at my gig at the Grange Hall? You can play your guitar and maybe mandolin on a couple of tunes."

Jason had hung out so much with Scratchy, playing guitar as he shared his songs, that he knew many of them by heart. He had even tried some of them on mandolin, which really impressed Scratchy, despite his protests that he was just learning to play it. In the process, they often shared a couple of quarts of Tumwater beer, but Scratchy wasn't the

Accidental Destination

kind of guy who readily shared the stage. "Why should I get up there with someone else?" he once said to Jason. "That just takes up more time playing extra verses without words. If I ever have a band, I think I'll call it The Interchangeable Parts—Peter Lohi and The Interchangeable Parts."

"That's rude," Jason said. "I wouldn't want to be an interchangeable part."

"No, no . . . it's not rude. It reflects the world as it is. It's like Henry Ford and the assembly line. We're all interchangeable. You'll see."

"But even so," Jason replied.

The Grange Hall was known for its hard maple dance floor and stage with a thick, maroon velvet curtain that could be raised or lowered with the press of a button. The curtain was an embellishment added years after the hall had ceased to be a meeting place for Wobblies and other union organizers. It was Jason's favorite music venue. He had seen Pete Seeger, Hot Tuna, Country Joe and the Fish, and even Mose Allison perform there. And now he was going to perform on that stage with Scratchy—the same stage that some of his favorite music legends had stood upon. As Jason fell asleep that night, he imagined himself onstage, standing in the same spot where Pete Seeger had once stood.

But Scratchy didn't use the stage. He pulled two folding chairs to the middle of the floor. "We'll sit here," he said. "Help me set up some more for the audience." They put out forty-eight chairs, in two "aisles" of four chairs each, six rows deep. "That should be more than enough," Scratchy said. "If we need more, people can grab them as they come in." There were no microphones, no PA system, no setlist.

Jason and Scratchy sat down, tuned their guitars and warmed up as people began walking in. Many of them knew Scratchy and greeted him with a nod or a handshake before sitting down. Jason noticed that when Scratchy's arms rested on his guitar, he didn't twitch or scratch. At exactly 7 p.m., Scratchy stood up and said, "Hello, everybody. Thanks for coming out tonight. It looks like it's time to begin. I'm Peter Lohi and this is Jason. He's kindly agreed to accompany me on guitar and mandolin tonight."

The room got quiet. Those standing about found seats or moved quietly to the side. Before and after each song, Scratchy talked to the audience, often spending more time introducing the songs than it had taken to play them. And they hung on his every word, shaking their heads and chuckling in all the right places. After each song, the audience clapped more enthusiastically than Jason thought warranted, given the informality of the "concert."

Before they started playing, Jason had been nervous, wanting to give his best performance, but now that the show was underway, it didn't seem like Scratchy or anyone else was paying attention to him. They were all focused on Scratchy and, as the concert progressed, they acted like they were hanging out in Scratchy's living room, asking him questions or calling for requests when Scratchy was trying to decide what to play next. Jason strummed and fingerpicked softly in the background, willing himself to be invisible, trying to unobtrusively add texture and depth, focusing on the content of Scratchy's songs, rather than the music itself.

"Before I play one last song, I'd like to thank the Emerald Folklore Society for asking me to open the show this evening," Scratchy said. "I'd like to thank them for publicizing this event, and I'd like to thank you all for coming out to see me. And please give Jason a big hand for coming out and supporting me tonight."

And they did. I have to hand it to Scratchy, Jason thought. He can turn on the charm when he wants to. Jason felt a real warmth, a sincerity, from the applause. He smiled and gave a quick wave of his hand. He had encountered a boosterism here that extended to just about every autoharp and dulcimer player in town, but this was the first time he had experienced it personally. He sensed that people stereotyped him as coming from The Big City, as someone who—as soon as he opened his mouth—didn't blend in with their down-home folksiness. This warm reception was unexpected. Jason put his arm around Scratchy's shoulder and the applause grew even louder.

Jason thought back to his New Jersey gigs—the cramped stages, the smoky rooms, the rented PAs, the toll roads, the obnoxious boozers. *You suck!* was the default cry if someone in the audience didn't like you. Once, in some corner dive, some guy had yelled out *Jukebox!* when Jason asked if there were any requests. The few who dug what he was doing, sitting quiet and attentive near the stage, hardly made it worthwhile. No, he didn't need any more of that. He was going to—well . . . not do that again.

But this? This was so . . . *insular.* "Thanks, everybody," Jason said as he tried to bend at the waist to take a bow with Scratchy, but Scratchy stood immobile, erect, as if he didn't feel Jason's gesture.

"And now," Scratchy said, "it's my pleasure to introduce to you a great group who drove in all the way from the coast to be here this evening—Shanty Tide." More applause. Four men got up from the audience and grabbed their instruments: a concertina, mandolin, hand drum and some tin whistles. With their striped T-shirts, sailor's caps, neckcloths and loose-fitting jerseys, they looked like they could have stepped off a nineteenth-century sailing vessel. Are these guys for real? Jason wondered.

"Wearzmuh guitah?"—*Where is my guitar?*—he heard one of them ask another.

"Weardjaleavit?"—*Where did you leave it?*

Don't blow your cover, guys, Jason thought. And yet, when they began performing, they sang with the richest seafaring brogue Jason had ever heard live.

Scratchy kneeled at the back of the room, quietly packing away his guitar in a cardboard case covered with stickers. He even had a couple of stickers on his guitar. Jason walked over to him and said, "Hey man, thanks. Thanks for asking me along. This has been great."

"You're welcome. And you were great," Scratchy replied. "You didn't jump all over the songs like you usually do in our living room. You tend to play too many notes, like a drunken Earl Scruggs. It takes restraint to be a good accompanist, and you were in the sweet spot tonight."

At that moment, Jason realized that it *had* been great.

He could see himself touring the Pacific Northwest—and maybe even up and down the California coast—as a Not-So-Interchangeable Part, playing rural auditoriums and tent shows at county fairs, laying low in the background, one of any number of band members. That would be the life. I could do that, he thought. A few more musicians, our own PA—a caravan, truckstops, 24-hour diners . . . I could definitely do that. We could sell homemade cassettes and maybe even autographed posters to pick up a few extra bucks. We might not make it big, but I'd be living the life— the music, the open road, the parties, the chicks—lots of chicks. That's what it's all about—the life.

But Scratchy was a lone wrangler, a vagabond tramping through life just as surely as the out-of-work, down-on-their-luck drifters in his songs. He had already crisscrossed the country looking for a place to settle down and this was it. *This* was his scam. Government checks and informal acoustic gigs in the middle of nowhere. The fuck-all was that Scratchy could be a national treasure, and, judging from the response of the audience, he was one of the only ones who didn't know it.

Jason rested his hand on Scratchy's shoulder and said, "Catch ya later, man. Thanks again."

7

TURN ON YOUR LOVELIGHT

Jason was inside the stadium. That much he knew. He was clutching a ticket stub, people were floating past him, paying him no attention. He had taken a hit of acid an hour and a half earlier, and now things were beginning to get strange. He touched his tongue to the roof of his mouth and felt a rough sweetness. Could a drop of liquid be responsible for all this? Objects were losing their solidity and undulating within him and without him. Sounds swirled around his ears. He looked at what he knew had to be his ticket stub, but he couldn't decipher the tangled hieroglyphics.

I'll walk through that flaming entrance in front of me, he thought. That fire isn't stopping anyone. Besides, the owls guarding the doorway won't let me through if that's not the way to my seat. Wait—I know I'm not supposed to be on the ground floor. I'll try that winding staircase to my left. He turned, but the staircase had already vanished.

Jason heard a woman's voice call to him from all directions at once, as if it were bouncing off the walls, floor and ceiling. "Hey-ey Jag-u-ar-ar-ar—How-ow aare ya-a-a?" A shimmering pillar of blue light moved swiftly toward him. It was Jenny, the flute girl, wearing a pastel crown of flowers.

Jason was melting—he'd stood too close to the burning door—he knew it—but the heat dissipated at the sound of her voice and was replaced by a cooling rush and the fragrance of roses and magnolia. Her smile kept sliding off her face like sand in a windstorm. She was surrounded by light—violets and turquoise blues and crackling flashes of saffron and gold.

"I'm OK, but I can't find my seat."

"Really?"

She obviously couldn't see the stairways wobbling around them, leading to . . . who knew where any of them led? His seat had to be up one of them, but the passageways kept shifting.

"Really."

"OK. Let's see your ticket." She said it with such concern, such gentleness. She wasn't going to leave him adrift in the lobby. Not her. "Mezzanine, Left, F-10 . . . OK—It's over this way. C'mon. It's just up these stairs." Her voice was a thousand flutes in harmony, simultaneously close to both the earth and heavens, like birdsongs in the mist after a drenching rain.

The crowd parted as she approached the stairwell. Jason trailed in her wake, his footsteps heavy, like lifting his feet in deep water. "It's right here—this one, right next to the aisle." She patted the back of the chair and took both of his hands in hers. "Maybe I'll see you after the show," she said. She winked, flickering in and out of focus. Jason's chest gasped for breath, a school of fish popped out and retracted like a Jack in the Box. "Let's meet in the lobby after the show," he heard himself sputter, his tongue a tidepool choked with damp sand.

"Sure." She smiled. "Maybe. We'll see." She flipped her head, as if trying to keep the hair out of her face, and was gone.

Jason turned toward the stage. It was oceans away and yet he felt as if he could touch it, if only he could stretch his elasticized mind a little further. He tried to walk toward it, but something blocked his way. A railing.

The stage was empty. Then it wasn't. Figures appeared, then disappeared. Sound flowed from it. Then it didn't. Someone must have set up that wall of speakers, but they couldn't have done it so quickly, could they have? Is that the band? The air was murky and pungent. This can't be the concert. Can it?

Jason leaned toward the stage. He drifted high above it. People surrounded him. He rested on the railing. The sound stopped abruptly. Intermission? Or were they just tuning up? People were whistling, screaming, clapping, twirling, swirling and whirling. A shooting star whizzed by and then became a beach ball. Lights flashed around him. He wobbled at the center of a rip tide. Excuse me. Excuse me. I've got to sit down. The wooden stadium chair became his anchor. Just ride it out. Ride it out. Everything's cool . . . It's all in the mind you know. Who said that? Things are slowing, glowing, flowing like they always do. Like they always do. *Look for* . . . That's not in my head . . . *a while* . . . It must be the second set. The tide rolled slowly in . . . *at the* . . . The roar of . . . *sail away from me* . . .

Music, buckling and bursting, bubbled in the air around him. Wave after wave with no let-up, cymbal overtones hovered above it all like cupolas . . . *row* . . . *row* . . . *row* . . . Molecules of sound, stacked and spinning, were floating around him in five dimensions . . . *row* . . . *row* . . . harmonics pierced the air like minarets . . . *all I said was come on in* . . . Prismatic synapses fired translucent. Simultaneous lights crackled. Peals of thunder rolled: Ba da dum . . . Bum Ba da dum Bum . . . *Not faaaade aawaaayyyy* . . . Silence. Uproar. Empty stage. Were they ever here at all? Houselights. Was I ever there at all?

It was easier finding the lobby than it had been finding his seat. Jason took a left at the stairwell, followed it down and made another left at the ground floor. Jenny was leaning against the painted cinderblock wall near the snackstand, sipping something from a paper cup. Their eyes met. That omnificent smile again. "Heeey yoou—theeere yoou aaare."

"Thanks, Jenny. Thanks for helping me find my seat."

She took his arm above the elbow and pulled him to her side. "My pleasure." She lightly touched the back of his head and slid her hand down his shoulder-length hair. "C'mon,

Jaguar. Let's get some fresh air."

"OK."

OK? That's it? *O-K?* Two letters? That's all he could force from his larynx? He had to come up with more than that. He slipped his hand into hers and looked into her eyes. She smelled like rain. And lilacs. Her eyes were blue, blue as the horizon, a blue blue magnified through her rimless glasses. "Your eyes are blue, Jenny—Darling Jenny. Darling Jen-ny. Why can't I write a poem as immeasurable as your eyes?"

"You're wasted."

"No I'm not."

"Your eyes are wide as saucers."

"Not so much. I was. Your hand feels good, so warm, so warm."

The night air enveloped Jason and returned him to an earth punctuated with pine trees and stars. Effervescent rain descended like glitter. Why had he never seen rain like this before? Had there ever been a night like this? Or was every night like this? I might be high, he thought, but this isn't the acid. I can see the world like this anytime I want to. I just need to slow my mind down and do it. It's all here. It's always been all here. I'm not imagining any of this.

Jason and Jenny sat under the attic eaves on his foam pad bed, their arms around each other's necks. "I need you naked," Jason whispered, the words involuntarily escaping. "I need to feel your skin all over me." Jenny's top was off. Moments later, the rest of her clothes were too. She was bare, except for the delicately carved soapstone dolphin hanging from her neck on a blue leather cord. The dolphin winked. Jason felt warmth, moisture, tasted plums, smelled lilacs, and didn't feel high at all. It's just that everything was more . . . *intangible*. Lightning flashed. The lights outside dimmed. Thunder crackled. The candle flickered.

"I need you, Jenny."

"I'm right here."

"I need to be inside you right now."

"Not yet. Not tonight. I want it to be real."

"It *is* real. It doesn't get any realer than this."

"Yes, yes—it does," she whispered. "I want you to want me for me." Jenny pulled the sheet over them. "I can't do it like that tonight, but come here—I'll take care of you."

Afterwards, she sat up. "I have to go now, but here, I have something for you. Something for you to remember this night by." She pulled a dark bamboo flute out of her canvas bag and rolled it slowly between her breasts. "This is for you. I made it myself. Whenever you play it, I'll be with you."

Jason immediately became hard again. "Oh—*Love-light*— come *here*," Jenny whispered. Jason embraced her, rocking back and forth in safe harbor, the sun rising on his mind's horizon, crickets chattering in the distance. He held Jenny tight as they moaned rhythmically, stuck together with sweat and desire. "Oh, Jenny, I—"

"Sssh . . ." she whispered, pressing her fingers to Jason's lips. "No talking now. There'll be plenty of time for that later. Just don't ever forget this night."

Jason was soon calling her Jen and she was calling him Jay. Most mornings began with Jenny blowing a few notes into one of her flutes. "I like to welcome each day," she told him. "I try to celebrate every one of them with a fitting melody. Today is a grey day. I like those the best."

One afternoon she handed him a joint of homegrown and asked, "Have you ever heard of The Sons of Champlin, Jay?"

"The Sons of Chaplin?"

"No, *Cham*plin. They're from San Francisco, my old hometown. Here—" She pulled out a record and handed him the cover. He stared at the hand-drawn neon-colored letter-ing as she placed it on the turntable. *Loosen Up Naturally*. There was a line drawing on the double album cover of . . . *something*. And the inside got even weirder. The music was trancelike, but with a horn section. Jason had never heard a big band so tight that could get this far out. It was lovemak-ing music and Jason was in love. That universal love, ignited by a human partner, a mystery that transcends the flesh and brings supreme peace and divine unity with the cosmos.

Or maybe it was the weed. What did he really know about Jenny anyway? Not that she was *secretive*, but some things never came up. And what did she know about him? "I know all about you, Jay," she would say whenever he questioned her. "I know everything I need to know about you."

That evening they snuggled, flipping through an old photo album of hers. Jason saw that not too long ago Jenny had had long hair. "Wow . . . your hair! What happened? Did you get tired of being so beautiful?"

"No. I got very sick and they had to cut it off. But I'm OK now. I think. We'll see. Don't—let's not think about it."

The next morning, she didn't play her flute at sunrise. Instead, she scrambled him some eggs and peppers in a small cast-iron skillet. "Do you realize this is the first time you've ever cooked anything for me? Jason asked.

"I'm not much of a cook. I've never really had to be. This is the closest I have to a specialty." She sliced and buttered a loaf of French bread, spooned the eggs and peppers inside it, and set the sandwich on a plate on the table in front of him. She pointed to a small silver salt-and-pepper set. "Salt and pepper to taste," she said.

"You're not eating?"

"I'm not that hungry. I like to watch you eat." She sliced a peach and ate the slivers one by one, watching in silence as Jason devoured the sandwich.

"Thanks. I was really hungry."

"I know. You can always eat. I like that about you."

Birds chirruped outside the window. He wiped his hands on an oversized linen napkin.

"Jason—"

Oh no, he thought. She never calls me that anymore.

"Jay, listen. I hate to spring this on you this way. . ."

Oh no. Is she breaking up with me?

"There's something I need to do . . . I have to take care of something back home. I have to go away for a while, but I'll be back, OK? You know I love you, Jason. I'll always love you."

"Jen, I . . ."

"Shhhh, now. I had another life—a life that doesn't belong to this one. I don't want it messing us up."

She threw her arms around him and gave him a long, passionate kiss, then pulled his head back and stared into his eyes."Just hang in there and trust me—I'll be back. I promise . . . I'll be back."

Jason must have walked past Jenny's apartment dozens of times on dozens of days. Weeks passed. The sky regularly became overcast and it rained at least a little each day, but Jason noticed few people carrying umbrellas.

He finally knocked on her door. A woman he didn't recognize answered and said, "She moved out. I didn't know her. The manager might know where she went to. Maybe she's got some sort of address."

Jason realized that he had no other address for her either. He didn't think he'd need one. She said she'd be back. She *promised* she'd be back. And here I am standing drenched in cold rain like a supplicant. Is this how our time together ends, so unceremoniously? Was our love nothing more than a hallucination as fleeting as the days and nights we held each other in our arms?

8

THE ACID BUST

If you asked Jason, he'd tell you that he didn't deal drugs and that he had never dealt drugs. Oh sure, maybe sometimes he'd bought more pot than he needed, he'd share it with his friends and they'd reimburse him—but he didn't *deal*. Once, he bought a quarter pound of Mexican (it was cheap enough) for his own personal use, to see what it felt like to have that much stash all at once. He'd hollowed out an old book to keep it in, but he was uncomfortable having that much weed around the house, so he sold some to a friend. But he didn't *deal*.

These days, a batch of really good acid was floating around Emerald. It was cheap and pure and came in those little plastic bottles with thin, molded droppers so that you could squeeze out a drop or two at a time. The liquid hit the tongue like rainwater and left no sugary aftertaste.

One afternoon, McCann squeezed a drop into Jason's mouth as he was leaving the Anthill and said, "Check this out. Let me know what you think." Jason spent the next twelve hours at one with the universe and he couldn't help telling his friend The Professor back in New Jersey about it the next time they spoke on the phone. The Professor had earned his nickname by dropping out of an Ivy League university during his second semester and saying *higher education* whenever he made a point involving drugs, which he did frequently. He could be pedantic, but he was the undisputed brains of the outfit, having logged more time in school than Jason or any of his friends.

"We could use some of that out here," The Professor said. "We should do a deal. It'll be easy—you'll make a few bucks and we'll have some good stuff around here for a change. We'll start out small . . . say 2,000 hits. Find out what it costs and I'll get the cash to you."

Holy shit, Jason thought. This guy's got it all figured out already. What am I getting myself into? I'm not a dealer and I'm not an acidhead. I only do it occasionally.

Pot was a different matter. It was just something he and his friends did. They barely gave it a thought. It was no big deal, although Jason couldn't name a single person any of them hung out with—with the exception of Maz, a poet back in New Jersey—who didn't smoke every day. Maz smoked occasionally, which meant that he smoked whenever Jason and his friends were around. And while they didn't give pot much thought, LSD was a different matter. They stopped short of calling it a sacrament—that would have taken the fun out of it—but it was a sign, a password to a community of like-minded individuals. To Jason and his friends, there were two kinds of people in this world—those who had tripped and those who had not. You didn't have to do it a lot, but you had to have done it at least once.

Jason remembered the acid trip he had taken with Maz and The Professor back in New Jersey. It was Maz's first trip. He had to be coaxed into it with references to William Blake and visions of angels materializing unbidden in the clouds. But he was a friend, a writer, a published poet—in short, a prime candidate, someone who needed to be brought into the fold.

They had been visiting Maz in his dorm where he was celebrating the end of his first semester at a state college. Until he swallowed his tab, it was uncertain whether he would partake or not. But swallow it he did, so Jason and The Professor swallowed theirs. As they waited for the acid to kick in, Maz politely kept answering The Professor's solicitous questions about whether he was "feeling anything yet."

Accidental Destination

Just as Maz was giving up hope of the drug having any effect whatsoever, The Professor picked up a copy of the *Live Dead* album and placed it on the turntable to play "Dark Star." As the first few measures began, the bass and guitar sounded like a full orchestra to Jason. The Professor handed the cover to Maz. "Whoa—" he exclaimed. "The coffin and woman burst off the cover. It's like it's in three dimensions. I never *got* the cover before. Now I *really* see it."

"*Now* you know," The Professor intoned, nodding his head sagely.

The dorm room on a Friday night was a little too unsettling for these three heads full of acid. Drunken students yelled down the hallways, funk and country music competed with the Dead, blaring through open windows and seeping through the walls. Maz's roommates were watching a comedy show on television in the living room and sounded like porpoises when they laughed. The walls wriggled like funhouse mirrors. The smell of unwashed laundry and pizza crusts filled the room.

"This is neither the proper set nor setting for this," The Professor said. "Is there somewhere else we can go?" Jason wasn't sure what *set nor setting* meant, but getting out of there sounded like a good idea.

"We can walk to the duck pond. It's right next to campus," Maz said.

The air was warm with a trace of humidity. Jason felt the air part with each step, a damp breeze cradling his head. The pond appeared as a large, shimmering disk before him. Mist rose from the water, dew rested on the tall grasses. An egret stood poised, motionless in front of a flock of geese. Jason sat on the bank, feeling the cool earth through his jeans, inhaling the moist air, and tuning in to the zipping insects and the distinct calls of birds. The whoosh of car tires on asphalt in the distance sounded like spinning wind and blended seamlessly with the croaking of frogs.

Maz stood entranced by the geese. They craned their necks as they flexed their wings, rocking side to side. They finally took flight and Jason wiggled his toes as they formed a flying V, disappearing into the night sky. With the geese gone, time itself seemed to dissipate in their wake, superfluous.

The Professor broke the silence: "This is more like it. Allen Ginsberg said that one should only do psychedelics in a natural setting or with intelligent people."

I'm doing both, Jason thought, as The Professor's words bounced across the surface of the pond.

In due time, the three intrepid travelers decided to return to the college. They had not walked a block on the main road when a police car pulled up silently beside them and two cops with flashlights emerged.

Everything's cool, Jason thought. They can't see our minds. He had learned this from a Richard Fariña novel.

"What are you boys doing out here tonight?" the fat one who resembled Porky Pig with a mustache asked as he shined his light on them, panning it slowly, directly into each of their faces.

"We're just out walking," The Professor replied.

"And why would you be *just out walking*?" the mustache with the flashlight crackled.

"Nice night for a walk," Jason replied, as a blue blur hovered in front of him.

"Just out walking?"

"Yes, sir."

"Where you comin' from?"

"The duck pond," Jason replied.

"What's at the duck pond?"

"*Geese*," Maz blurted out, suppressing a giggle. Jason was surprised to hear Maz speak. And did he imagine that smirk on Maz's face? He was the quiet scholar, the polite, introspective one.

The cops turned toward Maz. "And who are you?" Mustache demanded, his flashlight hovering inches from Maz's face.

"I'm Jorgus Mazeweski. We're students at the school there," he said, flicking of his chin in the general direction of the college.

Mustache and Blue Blur glanced at each other and shook

Accidental Destination

their heads in unison. "You boys have a nice night," Blue Blur said.

The patrol car pulled away and The Professor said, "See—acid is like that. We all could smell those cops' bullshit a mile away. All you have to do is tune in and step behind them when they ask you something. It's obvious what answer they're looking for and you just have to give it to them."

The three intrepid travelers remained silent until a few minutes later when they reached the outskirts of the college. "*Of course* we looked suspicious," The Professor said. "We're in New Jersey, it's nighttime, and we were out walking."

Jason wiggled his toes at the memory as he stashed a few hits inside a greeting card. He mailed it to The Professor from an out-of-town letterbox in an envelope marked with a false return address. It never arrived.

"No—" The Professor said. "Use your *own* return address. Mail it from Emerald. Everything has to look just right."

Easy for you to say, Jason thought, but he followed instructions and this time the card arrived. When The Professor called Jason, he was ecstatic. "This is some great shit. There's nothing like it here. We can sell this for four, five, maybe six times what it costs us," he said. "For now, the mail will do, but when the deals get bigger you might have to deliver the stuff personally. If that means three days in on the bus and three days out right away without seeing any of your friends here, that's the way it's got to be. You'll need to fly in under the radar and keep a low profile."

This thing was taking on a life of its own. But Jason had committed and it was too late to back out.

Less than a week later, Jason received the cash—twice the wholesale cost—in a box camouflaged with several science fiction novels, sent media mail. "You've got to read Robert Anton Wilson," The Professor said when Jason called to say the money had arrived. "Feed your head. Grace Slick said that meant to read books. She's a *big reader*, you know. She believes in *higher education*."

The profit was enough to keep Jason afloat for at least another month. Whatever misgivings he had, evaporated.

Jason didn't know who exactly had introduced him to his connection—he was more of a friend of a friend's friend who Jason had come to know. Such "friends" were always coming and going at the Anthill. One night Jason had walked into the kitchen and saw some guys cutting up a brick of hash on the table. One of them offered Jason a taste as nonchalantly as if they were slicing a pound cake, rather than shaving a kilo of aromatic green resin. That word seemed appropriate now. *Connection*.

McCann had long red hair tied in a ponytail and a close-cropped beard. He usually wore a hand-woven Baja hoodie, clean new blue jeans and Birkenstock sandals. His toenails were immaculately trimmed. He could have stepped out of a "Hippies Are Us" catalog—a catalog not for *actual* hippies, but for consumers of a sanitized, more mainstream version. McCann rented a two-story duplex on the Southside—not exactly upscale—but it was the neighborhood that the artists and yoga instructors move to when they've grown up enough to have steady jobs and families.

Jason had already stopped by several times to discuss prices and delivery and such. He didn't feel any special affinity with McCann, but whenever he came over, McCann would invite him to sit in a sparsely furnished room with cushions on the polished oak floor and partake of whatever bud was being passed around with whoever else happened to be there at the time. Invariably, Jason became stuck to a seat cushion, paralyzed, staring out the second-floor window at the light dancing on the leaves of a weeping willow whose branches swayed close to the window. They should call this stuff *Couch Glue*, Jason thought, cupping the hand-carved pipe with both hands so that the moist bud would burn more brightly. I couldn't get up if I wanted to, which I don't.

Jason knew the difference between shake and bud, and took the claims of what was purported to be Colombian,

Oaxacan and Thai Stick at face value, but *these guys* . . . these guys agonized over the color, the diameter of the individual strands, the pungency, the stickiness . . . Jason couldn't follow the fine points of the conversation. To him a bud was a bud. The difference between Burmese and Purple Kush was lost on him, so he kept his mouth shut. Not that he could have said anything anyway. They examined entire *branches* with the buds still attached. And they did it as critically as agricultural students inspecting a new strain of corn. Any of these samples could have been a contender for the centerfold in *High Times* magazine. What a great place to get wasted.

One evening Jason dropped by, expecting to pick up the vials of acid. Delivery had been delayed a couple of times and now that it was actually here, McCann was standing in the doorway, eyes red, talking in slow motion like an announcer on National Public Radio.

"I couldn't say anything over the phone, but the price has gone up a bit. I'm going to need an extra $200 to do the deal."

"But that's not what we agreed on."

McCann shrugged with a single shoulder. "I don't control these things. That's just the way that it is."

"That's a rip-off."

"If that's the way you feel about it, then forget it," McCann replied.

"If that's what you want—fine," Jason said as McCann closed the door in his face.

The deal had gone on for so long and now it had finally unraveled. Jason had to tell The Professor. "These things happen and the price still isn't *that* unreasonable, everything considered," he replied.

"But it's fucked up."

"I know it's fucked up, but that's the price. Tell him you'll pay it."

But when Jason saw McCann again and asked him to do the deal, McCann refused to sell to him. "You called me a rip-off," he said.

"No. I didn't. I said the *price* was a rip-off." Jason didn't understand what the fuss was all about. All he had said was, *That's a rip-off*. It's not like I said, *You're a fuckin' rip-off*, Jason thought. "I have the cash on me," he said.

"I don't like being called a rip-off."

"I didn't call *you* that. I was just surprised that the price had gone up—that's all."

"If you don't trust me, that's cool. But I've never cheated anyone. It's bad karma. With me, everyone gets a righteous count. In this business, you have to develop a level of trust. I thought we had that."

"OK, man. I'm sorry. I misspoke." Jason crinkled his toes. Jeez, he thought, I didn't realize I was dealing with Yogi Do-Right here. In Jersey, it's always a single wrong turn into Rip City. "Don't cop out on me now. We're too far into this."

"Anyway, I only have half right now. This stuff comes from California and there have been some delays. If you give me the money for the whole thing, I can give you half now, and I'll bring the rest by as soon as I get it—a few days, a week, tops."

"No problem. Thanks, man." Now *I'm* thanking *him*, Jason thought. *And* fronting him the money. How the hell did I get into this thing in the first place?

"You're still staying with Scratchy?"

Jason nodded. "Yeah."

"I know him. He's a good guy. He likes his beer, but he's cool. Hang tight. I'll catch up with you as soon as I can."

A few days later, Jason and Scratchy were home, playing guitar. Scratchy was singing a song about a Mexican smuggler with a single-engine plane who flew low across the border no questions asked, because he needed the money to feed his family.

Scratchy finished the song, rested his fingers lightly on his knees and said, "Did you hear about McCann? He got busted last night with a thousand hits of acid. The cops were waiting for him at his house. He stopped by here yesterday afternoon looking for you, but you were out."

9

THE NOT-SO HANDYMEN

I coulda been busted and for what? For all I know,
McCann wasn't even busted and this is all just one big rip.
"Enough of this," Jason said one rainy afternoon as he pol-
ished his guitar in Marshall's house. "I need a regular job."

"You should apply for CETA," Tim replied, cracking open
another quart of Tumwater. "I did it a few years ago and
they set me up with a gig making cabinets. It was good for
six months." He pulled *Pronounced 'Lĕh-'nérd 'Skin-'nérd*
from its sleeve and slapped it on the turntable. "I was working there and 'Free Bird' came on the radio. The album had
just come out. I cranked it up and set my ear right next to
the speaker. Ronnie liked it *loud*. 'We *love* your ears,' he'd
say. 'We want to get *all the way* in them.' I think I lost some
hearing from the power saws there."

The Comprehensive Employment and Training Act,
which everyone called CETA, was a federal program that
Jason believed was designed to do exactly what the name
promised. Steady work was scarce in Emerald, but even
with the logjam of applicants, Jason breezed through the
intake process using the same scam mentality he had honed
applying for unemployment and food stamps. Maybe being
on food stamps worked in my favor, he thought. But how I
got offered a spot on a home repair crew is anyone's guess.
Maybe it's because I said I'd like to work with my hands to

create something of lasting value someday. Who knows?

But he had also told his caseworker that he'd never owned a tool belt or used a power saw, so the likelihood of his success—that is, of landing an unsubsidized job through anything he might learn in this program—must have seemed minimal to her. Maybe long-term success wasn't the goal. Maybe home repair was the only track going—a scam on the part of the government to keep the chronically unemployed occupied for a period of time, tweak the soaring unemployment rate a fraction of a point lower and pump a few bucks into a tottering economy.

Or maybe it's just one more example of bureaucratic mismanagement and another Government Tit for me to suck on, Jason thought.

But whatever the case, he didn't find himself intimidated by the skills or mental acuity of his fellow trainees. Lenny had *special needs,* and before they had even pulled out of the parking lot their first day on the job, Bob, the crew boss, pulled the rest of the group aside and told them not to joke around or roughhouse with Lenny because he might shut down completely. "He's not all there—if you know what I mean. If he says he has to go to the bathroom, stop and find him one right away—or else he could get really sick."

"So, it's our job to find him a bathroom?" Dirk, another trainee, asked. Dirk was on a work-release deal from county lock-up. "I guess we're *all here* because we're not *all there,*" he added.

A few days into the training, Jason suspected that the crew bosses might also be in some sort of program. Bob, a skeletal non-drinking alcoholic—a fact that he disclosed to everyone the first chance he got—was quickly dubbed *No-Booze Bob.* If he heard himself being called that, he'd half wink, nod his head up and down and raise his coffee-filled thermos in a mock toast. The other boss, Hank, was a former treeplanter who resembled a blond Santa Claus—if Santa wore bib overalls and waterproof construction boots and was taciturn rather than jolly. "Tree planting is a holy profession," he had said as part of his introduction, "but you can only do it for so long. Being out there in the elements and helping Mother Nature replenish her bounty . . . Aaaah." He seemed to exhale a lungful of imaginary mountain air as he spoke, and, rather than continue, he stopped speaking and looked off into the distance as if *Ah* were the most eloquent statement possible, one that summed up exactly what he was trying to express.

Hank headed up a second crew that worked in tandem with No-Booze Bob. Everyone called Hank *Hoedad Hank*, or just plain *Hoedad*, after the treeplanting tool. Before even a week had passed, Jason felt like he was surrounded by an incongruous band of jesters, including the crew bosses, who didn't know whether they were ringleaders or roustabouts.

But that first morning, before he had met No-Booze Bob and Hoedad Hank, before he had been introduced to his coworkers, as he waited in the downtown parking lot, sipping coffee from a styrofoam cup, wondering what skills he might pick up during his training, Jason was enthusiastic. Maybe I can learn something to help me fix up my own house down the road—if I ever get one, he thought.

It was beginning to drizzle, so he buttoned up his denim jacket as he watched a bright orange pickup pull into the parking lot. No-Booze Bob hopped out and began distributing toolboxes and rain gear to Jason and the other members of what quickly became known as the No-Booze Crew. The rain gear consisted of a thick plastic slicker-and-pants set that fit over their work clothes. They were nearly identical to the ones Jason had seen Vodka wear at the Anthill when he headed out on his treeplanting expeditions.

The toolboxes all contained a claw hammer, a pipe wrench, a few screwdrivers—all the basics. "Hey—we got a monkey wrench in here," Jason said, pulling a tool out of the box.

"It's called an *a-djus-ta-ble* wrench," No-Booze Bob replied, slowly enunciating the syllables.

"I can't use this one," Dirk yelled, holding up his own wrench. "It's left-handed."

No-Booze squeezed his eyes shut and shook his head,

pressing his lips together, looking like he couldn't decide whether to laugh or scream.

The work consisted of banging out free home repairs for low-income individuals who themselves had applied for the *assistance*. Jason went out on many small jobs, but rarely repeated any one type, whether it was replacing cracked windowpanes, caulking a bathtub, changing out a toilet flap or installing a handrail on a front porch. He wore his rain gear more often than he thought he would. He crawled under a house and stapled lengths of pink insulation between the floor joists. "I'm not sure about this," he said. "I think this stuff might cause cancer."

"No way," No-Booze replied. "This stuff is totally safe. It's just fiberglass, the same as my cigarette filters."

Jason crinkled his toes inside his sneakers.

One afternoon he removed and replaced a toilet after cutting out the rotten wood underneath. (Actually, he watched while he handed No-Booze the tools to do so and the other crew members gathered around.) "This is too much for any of you," No-Booze said. "I'll show you how it's done." He hoisted the toilet easily and set it on the wax ring as gently as tucking a baby into a cradle. He's good with his hands, Jason thought—you have to give him that—but he's not much of a teacher.

Jason's biggest job was tearing off and replacing a roof. This turned out to be a three-day job. He liked being on the roof and was surprised at how easy it was to gain traction and walk around, but he didn't like tearing off the old shingles. "It looks like there's five layers on here," he said, as he pulled them off with a crowbar and watched clouds of dirt rise when he threw them in the dumpster below. "Are you sure none of these are asbestos?"

"Just be careful not to breathe it in," No-Booze replied.

The best part of the job was kneeling on the roof and hammering shingles onto the fresh plywood. The placement of the shingles and the arc of his swing soon became routine, and he thought about Jenny, her choppy blonde hair, her infinite blue eyes, her fish kisses, her arms and wrists thin as matchsticks. He had an address in San Francisco where she might still be. He had weaseled it from her old landlady. How pathetic he must have seemed. "I won't be the one to stand in the way of true love," she had said, as she handed him that scrap of paper. He hadn't expected the grey-haired old biddy to come through. How long ago was that? Jason wasn't good at keeping track of time, but he felt the days slipping by. If I'm gonna go see her, I'd better hurry up about it, he thought, pulling a roofing nail from his mouth and banging another shingle into place.

That afternoon as Jason was driving the crew back to town, Lenny whined, "I haave to peee." They were still some seventeen miles from Emerald.

"No problem," Jason replied. "I'll just pull off the road here. There's plenty of trees and bushes. You can take a leak over there, can't you?" Lenny didn't say anything. He just got out and walked quickly away from the van. "Anyone else?" Jason asked as he climbed out of the driver's seat. The others followed and found their own spots, then hung close to the van, stretching their legs. Dirk lit a cigarette. "C'mon guys, let's get a move on it," he said. "It's almost five o' clock. We need to be back downtown by then."

Jason and the others climbed back into the van. "Everyone all set?" Jason asked as he fired up the engine, turned the steering wheel toward the road and hit the accelerator. But the rear tires spun in the wet dirt and the van didn't budge. "OK. No problem. You guys get out and push—I'll drive." His coworkers managed to rock the van forward and back a bit, but the wheels splashed mud and dug deeper into the soggy earth. What a bunch of wimps, Jason thought, as he shifted into *park* and stepped out of the van.

At that moment, a compact car slowed down, backed up and swung in behind them. A Marine in blue dress uniform jumped out and asked, "Need some help?"

Jason noticed the perfect crease of his pants and impossible shine of his patent-leather shoes. "Yeah. We're stuck."

"I can see that."

"We could use some help."

"On it," he replied, as he grabbed a fistful of fir branches that were lying on the ground and wedged them in front of the rear wheels. He went for more branches and was getting close to a wet spot. Jason opened his mouth but words didn't come out. The Marine looked at the spot, glanced at Jason, grimaced, then grabbed more branches from another area. He moved like a machine—all business. He got behind the van and yelled, "OK—now put it in low gear and try it." He hunched over, put both hands on the bumper and pushed while Jason gently pressed the gas and the others stood back. The tires slid effortlessly out of the ruts.

"Thanks," Jason called out through the driver side window.

The Marine tightened his torso. "Roger that." He hopped back in his car and was driving away before Jason could say anything more. Jason was astonished that this guy would jump in and help, so impeccably dressed, and then could emerge from the embankment looking squared away and ready for inspection.

"Not too shabby for a ratfucker who shoots old ladies and children in Vietnam," Dirk mumbled as he crushed the last of his cigarette under his work boot.

"Shoots old ladies! Shoots old ladies!" Lenny yelled in the direction of where the car had been.

"Hey—" Jason said, "He didn't have to stop to help us."

"Yeah, and he didn't have to enlist either," Dirk replied.

Jason enjoyed his job, even as he felt the clockwork routine, the eight hours a day, five days a week, leeching a big chunk out of his life. There was something exhilarating about riding with this ragged crew that he couldn't put his finger on. Each day brought a fresh experience—stopping for coffee at some roadside café, meeting new people, driving on county roads to small towns—hell, Jason even felt like he was in charge of the orange van now. And it wasn't like they worked him to death. It was just a matter of showing up and driving where he was told. No Booze took over from there.

And the feel of that paycheck in his hand . . . Every other Friday afternoon, No-Booze would hand Jason a paycheck. He could smell it through the sealed white envelope. He'd stare at his name through the cut-out hole and imagine standing at the teller's window and watching her count out the cash, place the bills in a bank envelope and slide it across the green marble counter to him.

Jason splurged on a used car, a ten-year-old Ford Galaxie 500 that looked nearly new. It resembled a rocket-ship designed by a surfer—eight cylinders, a white-and-red two-tone paint job with tufted red interior, spoke rims and the suggestion of fins. Jason had never seen anything like it. Not in New Jersey, not anywhere. It looked like it had been garaged by a little old lady from Springfield. Not a trace of rust. And the price was right.

"This is the car you want," the mechanic who was selling it said. "It's a sweet ride—I checked it out myself. I even changed the oil for you." He popped the hood, pulled out the dipstick and placed it under Jason's nose. "Have you ever seen oil this fresh before?" Jason had to admit that he hadn't. He didn't know a dipstick from a radiator hose.

Jason had never seen anyone so enthusiastic over fresh oil. So ya changed the oil, he thought. Whadaya want—a medal? He handed over the cash, thinking that people here are as unpolluted as this oil. That's cool, but I gotta be careful not to lose my street smarts.

Days and weeks ran together, the rain began to let up, the training period ended, and Jason found himself back downtown sitting in front of his caseworker's desk, wondering what the next step in the process would be. He'd spent six months on the No-Booze Crew, and while he had a clearer idea of the technical aspects of home repair—he now knew what a *joist* was and he had seen the skeleton of a house being framed and wired—but he couldn't pound a nail any straighter or putty a window any smoother, no matter how much time he took.

Jason felt cheated. For all his scamming and talk of making it as a musician (and his secret dream of making it as a poet), he felt a real chance had slipped through his fingers— or rather he had never even been given a chance at this so-called *employment training*. None of them had. None of them had handled a power tool the entire time. Good thing too, Jason thought. Can you imagine Lenny with a Sawzall? He'd probably cut his arm off. I'll be OK, but I wonder what's next for him. Maybe this is all the future holds for me—eking out a life on the margins and nursing half-baked dreams I'll never see.

As his caseworker was opening his file, Jason tried to catch her eye. "Let me ask you something—How'd you get your job?"

"I have a master's degree in psychology."

Jason waited for her to say more, but she looked at him with a brick face as if this had fully answered his question.

And *I* don't, Jason thought. Got it. You can give me a spin on this merry-go-round and then transfer me to a fancier carnival ride, but that's about it.

It occurred to Jason that his caseworker might think he belonged here. I'm probably nothing more than a *case* to her, he thought—a statistic, one more number in a column of numbers to be tallied and crunched. I bet she runs us all through here like human ones and zeros. We're nothing but pawns to her—not even pawns—checkers, indistinguishable from all the other checkers she pushes around the board every day.

I'd rather be a poet or an itinerant guitar picker than cooped up like her in this windowless cell, an interchangeable cog in a business suit. She's not that much different from Hoedad or No-Booze—except for her fancy degree and the fact that she dresses better. I bet she's really smart, though. Which makes it even worse. She's just another people pusher who will do the shuffle here until the funding runs out. In a way, we're both on the dole. If I'm a checker, she's a pawn. Yeah—better a vagabond, with no direct power, no matter how minor, over anyone's life but my own.

"Do you need a master's degree to get your job?"

"Yes. Here's what I can do," she said. "I can set you up with a job at Lasting Impression Litho, the print shop downtown."

"How does that work?"

"We pay half your salary for the first six months with the understanding that they'll keep you on after that if everything works out. They also get a tax break for the next six months. We've got a few details to work out—You'll have to meet with the owner and he has to OK you, but if all goes well—and I expect it will—you can start in two weeks."

"That sounds good."

"To be quite honest with you Jason, this is a much better placement than we usually get. It's a good company. And they pay well. You'll be getting a nice bump in salary. Please make the most of this opportunity."

She looked directly into his eyes. "I mean it. They can fire you at any time, for any reason. As a friend, I'm telling you—don't screw this up."

10

ROAD TRIP

Jason had itchy feet and two weeks before he started his new job. If I hop in the Galaxie and take off down I-5, I can make it to San Francisco in about eight hours if I only stop for gas, he thought. Why haven't I heard from Jenny? Not even a postcard. Didn't we have a good thing going? There's got to be something going on. Maybe she's got another man. What am I—fuckin' crazy? I should just forget about her.

Jason hit the on-ramp shortly before midnight. That way he'd get there sometime in the morning and wouldn't have to spring for a motel, not that he'd stay in one anyway. All he had was a maybe address—not even a phone number. Well, he told himself, no big deal. It's a relatively short trip and I have the time. It'll be nice to get out of Emerald for a few days, no matter what happens.

Accelerating to highway speed was intoxicating. The smell of the night air, the river of highway that led anywhere he chose to go . . . Minutes melted into miles, and when he saw the lights of a 76 truckstop in the distance, he glanced at his fuel gauge, noticed he was low, and pulled off at the next exit.

Jason loved truckstops—the rigs lined up with their engines rumbling, the CB chatter, the chrome, the cassettes, the press-on reflective letters and the racks of T-shirts with goofy sayings like "My House Has Wheels." The phones in each booth, the *This Section Reserved For Truckers Only* area, the large portions, the oversized plates, the scratched ceramic coffee cups and the constant refills. It was a road warrior's well-lit asphalt oasis.

Jason grasped the menu in both hands and flipped through the laminated pages, but he already knew what he wanted. "I'll have the cheeseburger and fries," he said as the waitress filled his coffee cup. He always had the cheeseburger and fries—unless he went for a mushroom-and-Swiss omelette with hash browns and rye toast. Either one always hit the spot.

"Thanks, hon," the waitress warbled as she took his menu. Jason flipped idly through the selections on the mini-jukebox in his booth. Conway Twitty, Ferlin Huskey, George Jones—mostly country, a couple of Elvis . . . who listens to this stuff? Hey—Neil Young's "Revolution Blues" and "See the Sky About to Rain." Maybe I can get away with "Sky." He dropped a quarter in the slot and hit E-4. I'd better play a country song too, so I don't get thrown out of here. Let me see . . . "Tonight the Bottle Let Me Down"— that's *gotta* be a good one.

The waitress set Jason's order on the table. The burger was big—bigger than the typical off-the-road burger, a square slice of cheese melted on top, served on an oversized bun, with a pickle wedge and tomato slice resting on a leaf of lettuce. There was even a small paper cup filled with slaw. Jason squirted ketchup from a red plastic squeeze bottle onto the steak fries. It was an American work of art.

This is my America, he thought, as he set the top bun on the burger and dug in. They don't advertise the coffee cups here as bottomless, yet they always remain full.

It was already late morning when Jason crossed the Bay Bridge into San Francisco. He didn't know what he had expected, but the city seemed dirtier, greyer . . . *grittier* than he thought it would be. I'd better head straight to Jenny's, Jason thought, as he pulled over to consult his map. There'll be time for sightseeing later. If this works out, I'll stay with her tonight and we'll make love all night long.

OK. It looks like it's not too far from Golden Gate Park. I'll just drive until I'm close and then I'll park and walk. Parking around here looks pretty bad. Not as bad as New York though, and I always found a spot there.

Concentrating on the directions he had scribbled, he headed down Geary. When he reached his cross street, he snagged the first spot he saw. This was the first time he had had to parallel park since he left New Jersey and his boat of a car didn't make things any easier.

OK, I'll just walk the rest of the way and take in the city, he thought. While I'm here, I'll check out Chinatown and City Lights Bookstore. I'm sure Jenny can show me where they are. This is supposed to be a romantic city. It looks more burned out than romantic to me, but Jenny can make any place magical.

Soon Jason stood in front of a multi-colored Victorian. He had never seen such colors on a house before. And the exquisite detail of the trim . . . She can't possibly live here, he thought. In Emerald she had a furnished room. *This* . . . This was imposing. He double-checked the address, then walked up a flight of stairs between two fluted columns that led to a landing paved with . . . *marble* tiles? The tops of the windows were done in some sort of abstract stained-glass pattern. From this height he could see the bottoms of the trees in Golden Gate Park.

He stood before a door that looked heavy enough to be a chore to open on a regular basis. It was protected by a fili-greed wrought-iron gate. He twisted the mechanical door-bell three times. He thought about turning around and walking away. He didn't belong here and neither did Jenny. The front door opened inward. A woman with grey-blonde hair eyed him expressionlessly. "Yes?"

"I'm looking for Jenny?"

"And you are?"

"I'm Jason. Do I have the right place? I knew her in Emerald. I came down here to see her."

The woman pressed a button and the metal gate popped open. "You knew my Jennifer? Come in, please. I'm Angela, her mother." As Jason pulled the gate toward him and stepped inside, he felt strangely at ease.

"Please—have a seat," she said, motioning toward a lemon-colored wing-backed chair. Jason sank into its tufts. "Can I get you something to drink? A snack? Make yourself at home."

Jason thought back to the first time he had seen Jenny at the Saturday Market and how she seemed a little too well put together for Emerald.

It would take an interior designer to explain what he saw, but he knew it was carefully understated—and expensive. Very expensive. The coffee table was crafted of some sort of olive-colored wood, with an Asian scene inlaid on the top, covered by a sheet of non-reflective glass. Its curved legs, cupped with brass casters, rested on what had to be a hand-woven Middle Eastern rug. He had never uncrated a table like this and the rug looked nothing like any rug he had ever seen anywhere. Each individual strand on this rug was distinct. And it was worn. People actually walked on it with no thought of preservation.

Jennifer's mother returned, carrying a silver coffee pot on a silver tray. The sugar bowl and creamer were also silver. Sterling. They had to be. Beside them was a stack of impossibly thin vanilla wafers. Jason felt as if he had stumbled into a T.S. Eliot poem—"The Love Song of Jason Alfred Whatthefock." Angela glanced at the rug. "My husband had that sent back when he was doing some . . . *consulting* in Persia. They were practically giving them away. But you didn't come here to talk about rugs." She sat down and began pouring a cup of coffee. "*So—Jason—*how *well* did you know my Jennifer?"

He involuntarily crunched his toes together. *Why is she using the past tense?* "Pretty well, I guess. I met her selling flutes at the Saturday Market."

She took a deep breath, turned her head to the side and looked at the floor. "*Oh*, those *flutes* of hers."

"I came to see her. Is she here?"

Angela looked deeply into Jason's eyes, the same way Jennifer had done many times, except her mother's eyes were emotionless, quiet. "Jason . . . So you're the *Jay* she couldn't stop carrying on about." She set her coffee cup down and clasped her hands to keep them from trembling.

"Jason . . . I have some bad news . . . She's in the hospital . . ." Jennifer's mother shuddered and then the words came tumbling out, running together nonstop: "The specifics don't matter. All these damn diseases are bad. We thought she had it beat. We all hoped she had it beat. She went to Emerald, oh—I don't know why—hoping for, oh, I don't know what. Anyway, there was no stopping her—not that I could have, would have . . . She's in Saint Mary's now. You can walk there from here. You look like a walker. They recently opened it. You can't miss that crackerbox skyscraper. But the care there is top notch.

"But, why? Why didn't she tell me?"

"Who knows what that crazy girl of mine thinks? She probably wanted to spare you. We thought she had it beat. Then some more tests came back . . . and she had to come back here . . . for a . . . *procedure*. Maybe she thought, oh . . . I don't know what . . . Well . . . I'm sorry, Jason. I really am."

"I'm sorry too, Mrs. Hera. But I'm glad I know. I needed to know." Jason's breathing became shallow as he fought back tears. It had been a long time since he had cared to speak so respectfully to anyone so . . . *ancient*. I can't even talk to my own mother this way, Jason thought. We barely said goodbye when I took off for Emerald. But this woman makes it seem like there's no such thing as a generation gap. They both stood up at the same time.

Jason left in a daze. He began walking in the direction of the hospital. He cut into the park. So many roads and paths veered off from the entrance. He felt as if he had entered a labyrinth. He turned to the left. It was already late afternoon. I'd better get there before it gets much later, he thought. Otherwise I'll have to wait until tomorrow. He sat down on a bench and unfolded his map. Saint Mary's was marked with a small square. Let's see. I need to get out of this park—I should be close. I'll just ask someone. A man was about to pass Jason.

"Excuse me—" The man kept walking as if he didn't see or hear Jason. A couple was walking behind him. "Excuse me—do you know where Saint Mary's Hospital is?" The couple picked up their pace. The man avoided eye contact and as he breezed by said, "I have no idea."

What? Do they think I'm a panhandler? I'll just ask that cop over there. Jason didn't like cops. But if *you* approached them, he remembered Ginzo telling him, they were usually helpful because they wanted to get rid of you. If *they* approached you, you had to be on your guard. Ginzo liked to test his hypothesis by approaching cops and saying, "Excuse me, Lucifer . . ." and then asking them some bullshit question. Sometimes the cop's head would twitch as if maybe he hadn't heard right, but he always answered. Not that there was any reason for fear or suspicion in this case. But the strict marijuana laws had created a distrust of the police for an entire generation. *That* was the real generation gap—drugs. We are legal in every way, Jason thought, except that we can get sent away for years if we're caught with a couple of joints. Or at the very least, fined. Or hassled. We always have to be on our guard. That's something Jennifer's mother never had to deal with.

"Excuse me, officer . . ." Jason said to the helmeted cop maintaining a discreet distance from a group of transients who looked like they hadn't changed their clothes or showered in days. One was slouched on a rolled-up sleeping bag. Another was pulling a water bottle out of a hiker's backpack similar to the one Jason had landed in Emerald with. "Can you tell me how to get to Saint Mary's?" The cop's head swiveled a quarter turn, his right hand rested on his gun belt. He motioned with his free arm. "You can see it from here."

Jason nodded. "Thanks, officer." The cop remained impassive.

Jennifer's mother had been right. You couldn't miss it if you knew what you were looking for. It towered over the neighborhood.

Jason found Jenny's room easily. He told the nurses that he was her brother and they directed him right to her room.

The door was open. A tan curtain surrounded the bed and shielded her from view. He heard labored breathing. It was as if someone was straining to get their breath and then straining to expel it. He pulled the curtain back and saw Jenny propped up at a 45-degree angle, covered to the neck in a thin, synthetic blanket. She was hooked up to some kind of something. There were tubes in her nose, an IV, some sort of box . . . Could she be asleep or was this something else? A rosary was wrapped around her right hand. Mass and holy cards were arranged on the small table beside the bed. There were no silly get-well cards, teddy bears or flowers. "Jen?" Jason whispered.

Maybe she hadn't heard him. "Jen?" He leaned over the bed and took her left hand in his. It was warm and limp.

What am I doing here? he asked himself. He knew the answer, of course. This couldn't be the same girl who had tried to teach him to play her handmade flutes. "It's easy," she had said. "You just blow one perfect note, and then another. Then you let yourself go with the flow—always go with the flow." The way she had looked at him and laughed as if it were all so simple and he didn't have a clue. He'd settle for a smile right now.

He sat down on the chair next to the bed, still holding her hand. "Jen, you never let me tell you how much you mean to me, so I won't tell you now. But I'm here. And you know how I feel. I know you do. I'm glad I came down here to see you. Oh, Jenny. My Darling Jenny." He kissed her forehead and squeezed her hand. Did he feel a little squeeze back? If so, did she know it was him? "You really should have let me know." Jason placed his hand on top of her head, which was wrapped in a scarf. "Oh Jen, I wish you had said something." He stared at her closed eyelids, imagining the blueness beneath them.

I'd better get out of here, he thought. I don't want to have to explain myself to anyone. He removed the silver Saint Jude medal from his neck and wrapped it around the fingers of her left hand. "When you awake—and I know you will—you'll know I was here," he whispered.

Jason had long ceased to believe in any kind of religion,

but he wore the medal because it was a gift from his mother. She still prayed for him every day to Saint Jude, the saint of lost and hopeless cases. He patted the hand the medal now dangled from. "If anyone can help you, he can." He stood up and hurried from the hospital.

It was already getting dark. Jason had been up for nearly eighteen hours. He stopped in a storefront to buy a slice of pizza and realized he was on Haight Street. I can't believe I'm within walking distance of Jenny's house. This place is so trashed. What happened to the Summer of Love? Janis is gone. Jimi is gone. The Dead don't live here anymore. I'd better find a place to crash, he thought. I'll just drive around until I find somewhere I can sleep in my car.

On his way back to his car, he passed a music store and saw a beat-up, blonde Telecaster bass in the window. The bridge and string saddles were discolored and pitted, but its color reminded him of Jenny's hair. Jason had never played a bass before, but he knew he had to play this one. It felt like a piece of lumber resting on his leg. He tried to duplicate the opening riff to "Truckin," which he knew on guitar. The bass riff was similar to the guitar riff, just that the bass was tuned an octave lower. What he played was unrecognizable, but the first and last notes rang out like simultaneous sunshine and lightning. *These* were the perfect notes Jenny had been talking about. He kept hitting the octaves, letting the overtones ring out and then fade away.

Jason was hunched over the bass when he heard the salesman ask, "You gonna buy it or what?"

That's pretty fuckin' rude, Jason thought, but the bass spoke to him. "Sure," he replied. "I'll pay cash for it right now." He unzipped the pouch he carried around his neck and pulled out a packet of twenties. He thought he detected a brief look of astonishment on the salesman's face.

When he reached his car, he stashed the case in the trunk. It fit easily. This practically cleans me out, he thought. I hope I have enough for gas to get back. But I'd better find a place to get some sleep first. He drove until he found a spot overlooking the water and city lights. He could see a bridge. Fog was rolling in and he felt a chill in the air.

There were a few other cars here and there, but the place seemed isolated enough. Jason killed the engine. The world stood still, except for a few blinking lights in the distance. He inhaled deeply and closed his eyes. He heard a knock on his window. He opened his eyes and saw a policeman waving a flashlight. Half asleep, he automatically rolled down the window. "Yes?"

"Good evening, sir."

"Yes?"

"I'm sorry, but no one is permitted to sleep here."

"Was I sleeping? What time is it?"

"4:19."

"OK, officer. Sorry. I must have dozed off. Give me a minute."

The policeman touched the brim of his cap. "No problem. You just have to move your car—that's all."

Jason nodded his head in assent and the police officer walked toward another car. That was it? He didn't hassle me? He didn't check my ID? I guess some cops are just nicer than others. Or maybe he's *gay*. What the fuck. It'll be light soon. I might as well head back. This time I'll cruise up the coast highway.

Jason crossed the Golden Gate Bridge, heading north toward San Rafael and Highway 1. It hadn't occurred to him to stay in San Francisco another day. He wasn't thinking about Jenny. He wasn't thinking about City Lights or Chinatown. He wasn't thinking about anything in particular. He just wanted to hit the road and keep moving.

The highway began hugging the coast and it was slow going. It would be easy to pull off the road and walk onto the beach or at least get a good view of it, he thought. But what I need right now is some gas. I'm going broke keeping the gas gauge afloat. That's one thing that mechanic didn't warn me about.

He stopped at a market, filled his tank, and picked up some trail mix and oranges. He drove the twisted mountain roads that always wound back to the coast. So this is the coast, he thought. The *coast*—not the *shore*. No Convention Center, no Tilt-A-Whirl, no Madame Marie's or bootleg cassettes for sale. *The coast*. The sun was already beginning to flirt with the horizon and Jason wasn't even out of California yet. I think I'll pull over and watch one of those California sunsets that I've heard so much about, he thought. This would be a perfect place to fire up that joint I brought along. I'll just walk out on that—what is that—a *jetty*?

The rocks were solid under his feet, but it took longer than he thought it would to reach the end of them. Finally, Jason sat down, put the joint in his mouth, twisted it between his lips, and reached for his matches. Shit—no matches. He had heard of this happening, but it seemed more like a joke or an R. Crumb cartoon than a situation he'd find himself in. He looked back toward his car. Too far. Oh well, I'll just smoke it later. I don't need this to enjoy a sunset, he told himself. It would have been nice, though.

Jason sat on the rocks and watched the sky shift and the colors collide. The sun took its time slipping over the horizon—or was the horizon slipping past the sun? Whatever it was, it was breathtaking. Now he knew why so many houses here were painted in those impossibly delicate pastels. Those same shades came and went in the sky before him. This is it, he thought. The great equalizer. No matter who you are, we're all the same sitting before the ocean. We all might as well be naked as birthday babies—no IDs, no fancy haircuts, no rings or marks of distinction for all it matters to the rolling waves before me.

But it costs money to live here. It costs money to sit here and wipe the slate clean every evening. I wonder what Jenny's parents do. You don't get a house like that working in a print shop—or even owning one. I bet they were born into it. Or they're super scammers. I scam to live hand-to-mouth, but other people scam on a level I can't even imagine. What does it take to get one of these houses near the beach? I bet even Jenny's parents can't afford it. Maybe I could live here if I was a rock star. That'd be the only way.

I can see now why all those hippies dropped out to San Francisco. It's a beautiful place to build a dream. Now they look like they've all burned out and hit bottom. But what else could they do? Be a freak in some Midwestern town full

Accidental Destination

of straights?

But that's their trip. I've got my own life to live. I need to forget about Jenny. That's what she'd want me to do. It'd only ruin what we had if I play this out to the bitter end. Life's too short. My first order of business is to find a new girlfriend. A *real* girlfriend. Me and her, sailing together through life. What more do I need? I've already got a car, a job, a place to live. A bass. I've got a bass, my health and my whole life in front of me.

Now all I need is an amp. He laughed out loud and raised his arms above his head. "Go with the flow, man. Go with the flow," he intoned to the ocean waves before standing up and turning back toward his car.

INK IN THE BLOOD

&

BOARDING HOUSE FOLLIES

When Jason stepped into the pressroom his first day on the job, he inhaled the ink as though it were fresh air. The clatter of metal on metal was as refreshing as the waves of the Pacific. He felt the power of the presses surge with each revolution of the rollers and cylinders as pages wet with ink were spit out so fast they landed in their wire baskets with a ping. He saw the possibilities immediately. I need to get a press of my own, he thought. The pen may be mightier than the sword, but a press is mightier than 10,000 pens.

But Jason hadn't been brought in to run the presses. His bindery job consisted mainly of feeding paper through a machine that would fold and collate it, although some custom jobs were done by hand.

When his caseworker had asked him if he would like to work in a print shop, it hadn't occurred to him to ask, "Doing what?" When a hungry man is offered a sandwich, he doesn't ask what kind. Nor were his duties laid out when he was "interviewed" for the job. Rather than ask about

Jason's background and his suitability for the work, the owner—universally referred to as *the old man* (although never lovingly and never within earshot)—had eyeballed Jason and fired off a few perfunctory questions about where had he grown up and how long he had lived in Emerald. He shook Jason's hand and said, "Welcome aboard, son—and good luck." He then turned, steadied himself on his cane and walked back to his office. He closed the door, sat down behind his desk in a tufted leather chair, and peered at the pressroom through a sliding glass window.

At first, Jason didn't know that most of the printing jobs were for corporate newsletters, boilerplate contracts, business cards, letterheads and envelopes. And when he found out, he didn't care. He embraced the entire process—from the moment the job order entered the pressroom until it was stacked and ready to be picked up by the customer. He absorbed it all—how to paste up and shoot the boards, how to burn the plates for the press, how the images on the plates were reversed so they would print positive.

Once Jason got the hang of the simple machines, the bindery wasn't that demanding. Whatever paper had to be folded, collated, punched or bound, Jason did it easily. The secret was in the setup. If you set the machine up just right, the paper would run through smoothly.

But Jason wasn't interested in folding paper or punching holes in it. He wanted to put the ink on it. He wanted his clothes stained with ink, his hands worn raw from solvent, and his fingernails so blackened with ink that they would look like they always had dirt under them.

Jason loved the smell of ink. And the colors . . . The fact that just four colors—cyan, yellow, magenta and black could combine to produce any color in the visible spectrum fascinated him. He had read about this in books, but to actually see the colors mixed and roll off the press mesmerized him. There were so many colors that they had to be precisely designated by numbers rather than names like mauve, ecru, coral or Irish mist, which—as everyone knows—isn't really a color at all.

Between jobs, he was free to roam the shop as long as he

looked busy. It's the same everywhere, he thought. It's not enough to do a good job—you have to look like you're working every second and act like you're enjoying it. It's best to let the job expand to fill the time allotted, rather than to be efficient.

Jason would walk to the shelves where the paper was stored and rub his fingers over the textures of the various stocks and hold the watermarks up to the light. Sometimes he would talk to the girl who did the typesetting and admire the variety of fonts she had at her disposal. On slow afternoons, the pressmen would sometimes let him burn plates for them.

At first, the pressroom seemed huge, overwhelming, with so many different machines, paper stocks and cans of ink. But it didn't take Jason long to realize this was a small shop that contained only five presses: three small ones that accepted paper no bigger than 11x17, another that accepted slightly larger sheets, and a behemoth 4-color press, run by a specialist. The other four presses were up for grabs by the three other pressmen.

Running a small press is rudimentary if one knows how. Michael, who was a few years younger than Jason, had learned to run a Multi 1250 at his vo-tech high school. Jason watched him squirt a shot of liquid from a plastic bottle onto the press and wipe it off with the red rag hanging from his pocket. Right out of high school and already he had a trade and a good job. All Jason had learned in school—well . . . he didn't remember learning anything that would prepare him for a job.

He remembered sitting in the back of French class and flirting with this cute girl who was trying to get him to read a book called *Been Down So Long It Looks Like Up to Me*. She read a lot and every day she tried to turn him on to one author or another. I don't know how the teacher let us get away with it, he thought. That day she handed me a breath mint and the teacher came running to the back of the room practically screaming, "*Qu'est-ce que c'est? Qu'est-ce que c'est?*" I said, "A Tic Tac" and the girl held out the package for him to see. He said, "Oh, *un Tic Tac*," in a very nasally voice, then held the package up to the class, and waved it around saying, *"Les Tic Tacs, Les Tic Tacs,"* as if he were teaching us something. If I ever go to France, I'll have no problem ordering Tic Tacs.

Michael pulled a lever, the press stopped, and Jason picked up a broom to sweep up around the drill press.

Weeks passed. Jason worked the drill press. He swept the shop floor. He loaded boxes onto the van for delivery. He took his time setting up the folding machine and ran it as slowly as possible. He made scratch pads from paper scraps by brushing pink glop along the edges. If this is one of the better jobs CETA can set someone up with, he thought, I'd hate to see the other ones.

Jason didn't grumble about the paychecks though, and he soon realized that he could afford to move into his own apartment. I dig Scratchy, Jason thought. I dig having a guitarist around to jam with but when I come home from work, I don't want to have to talk to anyone, I don't want to see anyone stuff their face with noodles and ketchup, I don't want to deal with anyone else's dirty dishes in the sink—I need my own space.

The apartment that Jason found was not in a typical apartment building, but rather in a house divided into rooms with makeshift kitchens on the second floor, and two full apartments on the first. The plastic numbers nailed to the doors had been painted over so many times that they were nearly indistinguishable from the doors themselves.

Jason moved into a "studio" on the second floor and shared a bathroom with three other tenants, but this was the first time he didn't have any roommates. When he entered his front door, he stepped directly into the kitchen where a refrigerator, a stained porcelain sink and a grimy stove were crammed side by side against one wall. Chipped metal cabinets were nailed above them. The room also contained a yellow Formica table and two chairs with matching plastic cushions. The rent was cheap, utilities were included, and the window looked out on a small yard with a couple of mature plum trees.

Accidental Destination

Jason was glad to have his privacy. He had a good view. He was doing all right. This is not bad at all, he thought.

As he sat at the table, smelling the plum blossoms and eating an avocado sandwich, he heard a Hank Williams song waft so clearly through the heating grate that it sounded like it could be coming from the next room. "I-I-I'm so low-oh-oh-own-some I-I-I could cry-eye-eye." The woman's voice sounded more pitiful than plaintive. Jason walked downstairs and knocked on the door marked #1.

It opened, and a young woman looked up at him. She immediately smiled and Jason wiggled his toes. She wore a long colorful skirt, a fringed vest, red cowboy boots and clutched an inexpensive mandolin. She could have been an extra in a Western movie.

"Hi—I just moved in upstairs and . . ."

"Sorry if we were making too much noise."

"No, no, that's not it at all. I heard—that was Hank Williams, right?"

She extended her hand. "That's right. I'm Susie."

"Susie? Howya doin, Susie? That's gotta be short for Susan, right?"

"No—It's Susie. My name is Susie. It might have been better if my mother had named me Susan, but she didn't. You don't even want to know my middle name. Anyway, you wanna come in? It's Friday night and I'm having a little get-together with a couple of friends.

Jason entered Susie's portion of the house. The apartment was thick with smoke. An ashtray overflowed with cigarette butts. He wondered how three people could smoke so many cigarettes. Susie and her friends were drinking wine from thick red glasses. She handed an empty one to Jason. "My mom sent me these for my birthday last week. They're *really* expensive. We're breaking them in tonight." She poured Jason a glass from a nearly empty gallon jug of Burgundy. "The first one's on me. The rest you have to get yourself. Don't worry—there's plenty more. We never run out of wine around here. Have a seat. Make yourself at home." She sat on the edge of a bed that filled the entire alcove, delicately strummed the mandolin and picked up warbling Hank Williams right where she had left off.

Jason sat on an empty chair in the cramped passageway that led to the kitchen. Next to him sat a heavyset bearded man strumming a sunburst guitar that was much too red. This close, the song sounded ironic, as if Susie were mocking it. "You like Hank?" Jason asked the guitarist.

"We *all* love Hank," he replied. "Just *love* him to death." The words were accompanied by a puff of cigarette smoke. "Hi. Susie Mae here *insists* on calling me Stanley, but I still love her. All my buddies call me *Stosh—You* should call me Stosh," the guitarist said, delicately extending his hand. "I don't *really* play guitar, you know. I'm an *ac-tour*. And Sophie here next to me is studying costume design." Stosh was talking so fast that Sophie could only nod. "You should *see* her wardrobe," he continued. "It's *fabulous*."

Stosh reached for his wine glass. "Did you just move in upstairs? We call this place the Boarding House, although it really *isn't* one. It's just that people come and go like it is. Susie's been here six months. I think that's some kind of record. At least since that *horrid* gym teacher bought the place and kicked out all the old tenants so he could raise the rents. There was a nice old man who lived upstairs for years—he just gave him a month's notice and told him he had to go."

"Yeah," Susie said. "And the one time I was late with my rent and he came in here in his little tank top, all over me, flexing his muscles, saying, 'What can we do about this? We need to do something about this.'"

"And what *did* you do?" Stosh asked. "*Do* tell."

"I paid him a few days late."

"Are you *sure* that's *all* you did?" Stosh raised an eyebrow.

"Yeeuch—Not even if I was the Whore of Babylon."

"I would have been happy to help you out, you know, as a *personal* favor . . ." Stosh said, winking at Susie.

"And Jason, this is Sophia," Susie said.

"Call me Sophie," a pixie with shaggy hair highlighted in pink said to Jason. "I live in the apartment across the hall." She shook her head. "And don't pay too much attention to Stanley. He gets silly after a few glasses of wine."

"That's OK," Jason said. "He isn't bothering me."

"Oh, but *he's* bothering *me*," Stanley replied.

Jason noticed a thick book on the bottom of a bookshelf improvised with cinder blocks and loose boards. He picked it up with both hands. "Oh, *The Riverside Shakespeare*," he said. It was as heavy as the pages were thin. He had heard of it, but had never seen a copy before. A sticker marked *Used* was attached to the cover, which was full of scribbles. "Are you in the theater too?" Jason asked Susie. "No, I'm a whore." She laughed. "I just like to have fun. Can't you tell? No, really though—I'm a music major. Talk about a worthless field of study. The book is for a class I have to take at the university." Jason replaced the book. He took a gulp of wine and looked into her eyes. "You have a beautiful voice," he said.

"Don't you start with that," she said. "You seem like a nice guy. You don't want to get involved with me. I don't get involved with anyone. I love 'em and leave 'em. You're not my type anyway. I go for more muscular men."

In spite of her protestations, Susie let Jason fuck her one afternoon. It was about time. She'd been flirting with him whenever their paths crossed, although she also kept rejecting his advances. This particular day he had been sitting on the porch steps when she walked past him, lowered her sunglasses and said, "Well . . . hello there."

Here she goes again, Jason thought, nodding hello.

"Why don't you come in for a glass of wine?" she asked, and the next thing he knew he was on the bed in her alcove, his pants to his ankles and her dress pulled up to her waist.

Jason was immediately aroused. "Whoa . . . Susie. Susie—Slow it down will you?" He gasped for breath. No one had ever wanted him this fast, right here, right now. At least not anyone he had been attracted to. In the midst of it, the experience felt mechanical, as if she were going through well-rehearsed motions, scratching an itch—no more, no less.

But she knew exactly where to scratch. It was unexpected, refreshing, invigorating. It brought with it a freedom, a freedom not only to live in the moment, but a freedom from the seriousness and emotional attachment of Making Love, of wondering if this one is The One.

So this is *fucking*, Jason thought. Slam, bam, thank you, man. For all of our lovemaking, I never *fucked* Jenny. Not even once.

The next morning when they met in the hallway, Susie looked Jason in the eye and said, "Well I guess we won't need to be doing *that* again any time soon. But I like you. We should be friends. We just had to get that out of the way. I'm on my way to school to drop off a paper. Wanna come with me? I'll give you the grand tour."

The university might as well have been a different planet for Jason. It was so green, so vast, so intimidating. Ivy covered the older brick buildings, a modern library stood five stories high, as long as a city block. Weathered bronze statues and wooden benches rested in open spaces. Bicycles slid past with riders wearing daypacks. Jason tried to imagine himself as a student here. He could never get accepted, he thought. He had always been a lackluster student. He didn't fit in. But Susie, with her Western gal persona, didn't fit in either. And yet she seemed so comfortable, so confident, her head held high as if she were famous, expecting to be recognized as she glided through the crowd. "I should have been an actress in those old black-and-white Hollywood movies—like Ingrid Bergman or Katharine Hepburn."

Or maybe Dale Evans, Jason thought.

"Men would swoon. I wouldn't have to say a word. My eyes would do all the talking. I'd be a recluse, a mystery. I'd go out with a bang—or maybe age gracefully with a slow fade to black."

"You've got it all planned out I see."

"No. Not really. But I've had enough of reality. I'm looking for a good fantasy." The smell of her perfume mixed with the fragrance of her freshly washed hair as she put her arm around Jason's waist. "Thanks for last night by the way. I mean that. I know it was all about me. I did it for myself. I'm like that." She released her arm and stood facing him. "But, seriously, though—Sophia is the one you should be after. She really likes you, but she'd never say anything. Don't you say I said anything either. She's a real Girl Scout."

Susie laughed as they continued walking. "I'll be moving back home to Tucson the end of this semester. I'll probably meet someone there and get married. Or maybe I'll marry my high school sweetheart. He's still in love with me, you know. The Whore of Emerald gets roped, tamed and corralled as the sun sets on the saguaro. I'll probably end up fat with a bunch of screaming brats, too." She looked away, and, as if making a mental note, said, "But *first*—I'm going to get me some of that Marshall. He's a hunk and a half." She smiled and looked at Jason. "Now, don't you get jealous. And remember what I said about Sophia. She's more your speed. She could really use some of what you're packing, cowboy."

I'm getting dumped, Jason thought, but for the first time in my life, I'm enjoying it. An image of Sophia flashed in his mind. He had imagined himself with her more than once, but there had been no hunger, no yearning. He had hungered for Susie the way one hungers for an exotic meal. Their fire had burned hot but extinguished quickly like flambé. Jason had been nothing more than a snack and Susie had had her fill.

Sophia's a cute little thing, Jason thought. And if she likes me . . . I don't know . . . Maybe . . .

"Who knows?" he replied. "Stranger things have happened."

Jason noticed the bike racks in front of all the buildings. They were all full. He realized that Susie had parked on the outskirts of campus and they were walking in the middle of the street. "Where's all the cars?" Jason asked.

"Most of the campus is closed to cars. Pedestrians and bikes only. Wanna hear me play something?" She grabbed his hand and picked up her pace. "They've got a piano in the student center up there." She pointed to a building whose first-floor exterior was constructed almost entirely of glass that curved gracefully without any sharp angles. It reminded Jason of a fishbowl. The building sat at an intersection near the middle of campus. It was set back from the sidewalk, surrounded by a moat of bricks.

They passed a man shouting something about American imperialism in a post-colonial society. "That's the free-speech area," Susie said, as if sensing Jason's bafflement. "Anybody can get up there anytime and expound whatever cockamamie theory they want. The free and open exchange of ideas is critical to a democratic society." She sounded serious.

They walked up a curving flight of steps and turned left into the cafeteria. Students sat in booths next to floor-to-ceiling windows, reading, talking, eating. Others carried trays with cheeseburgers, fries, Taco bowls or plates overflowing with salad to their tables.

Jason and Susie passed through a hallway, up a flight of stairs and through a couple of rooms filled with leather sofas and chairs until they reached an area that looked like the other lounges they had walked though, except this one had a baby grand in the corner.

"Check this out," Susie said, as she sat down at the piano and pulled a worn folder of sheet music from her pack. The room was almost empty. Just a couple of students reading textbooks and a few more curled up on the overstuffed sofas. "This is the humoresque from Rachmaninoff's *Opus 10*." She rested her fingers lightly on the keys, turned her head to look at Jason and smiled that dismissive smile that was fast becoming her trademark. "OK now . . . Don't hate me for this." She counted off the piece with a few nods of her head and hit a flurry of syncopated chords that reminded Jason of Scott Joplin. Her fingers slid across the keys with no wasted motion, as if they were tiny ice skaters sliding on a river of ivory. The pages seemed to turn themselves with the mere flick of Susie's wrist, as if she were willing them not to interrupt the flow of the music. The piece became increasingly dissonant and then ended abruptly.

"Wow," was all Jason could say.

"Not as *wow* as you might think. That and 69 cents will get you a quart of your Boho beer."

Could this be the same girl who had so gleefully butchered Hank Williams the night I met her? Jason wondered.

Susie stood up from the piano bench. Jason picked up her music and handed it to her. "Who the hell are you?" he asked.

"That's a good question," she replied. "Who the hell are any of us?"

12

HARD PRESSED

&

THE VIET NAM ZIPPO BLUES

One day Jason asked Larry the foreman if he could learn to run the press. "We don't need another pressman," he replied. "We brought you in to work the bindery."

"I know. But maybe when there's no bindery jobs, instead of me standing around holding up a broom, you could cross train me."

"*Cross train.* Heh heh. That's good. Yeah. *Cross train.*" He pulled a Camel straight out of his T-shirt pocket. "I suppose it wouldn't hurt to *cross train* you. Sure, why not? Michael can do it."

"Hey, by the way," Jason said, "What's up with that tattoo?" Larry looked at the inside of his forearm as if he were seeing it for the first time. "I almost forgot about this. My buddies and I all got the same one when we were in Guam. Except I didn't get the 'Death Before Dishonor' part. I never went in for that bullshit."

Little by little, Michael began explaining the workings of the press to Jason, and although he was still not allowed to run it, he would sometimes secure the plates to the drum and pull the paper out of the basket after it had been printed. He was always careful not to jog the papers too roughly and smudge the wet ink.

As Michael was troweling ink into the ink tray he said, "When I was being interviewed for this job, the old man asked me what the most important thing about running a press was. I told him it was the ink-to-water ratio and I got the job."

"I don't know anything about presses," Jason said, "but I would have said 'the finished product.'"

"That's *true* . . . but I think he wanted me to show him I knew how to run a press. You're a funny guy. I'm surprised to see someone like you working here." Michael flipped a switch and papers slowly began sailing through the press. He grabbed a sheet as it left the drum and inspected it.

"I know. If I knew what you know, I'd have answered like you did," Jason said.

"I can dig it. It's ridiculously easy to run a press if you have the slightest bit of aptitude." Michael twisted a couple of set screws and pulled a lever. The press began running at full speed. "That's why these guys grunt and groan, trying to make it look so hard. They don't want anyone to know how easy it really is."

Soon Michael had Jason running the press on small jobs such as envelopes and letterheads. This usually involved him correcting Jason's set-up attempts, while explaining what he was doing. Then Jason watched the press run, fed it paper, added ink or wiped down the plate with solvent as needed.

When the press was running right, Jason grooved to the hypnotic beat of the cylinders as he grabbed a sheet and held it up to the light to inspect it or adjusted the ink-to-water ratio ever so slightly. Anyone who didn't know better would think Jason had mastered the capricious machine. Now, even when he was working in the bindery, he kept a red shop rag hanging out of his back pocket.

Every Friday afternoon, the shop printed and mailed a financial tip sheet. One day, Larry told Jason that if he thought he could handle it, he could take over the job. "You can set up the press and everything—Michael will watch you. Don't worry. As long as it's readable, they're happy. You'll also have to fold it, but you're already good at that, so you should have no problem."

The tip sheet was printed on an 11x17 sheet of 20 lb goldenrod, folded in half and then tri-folded and stuffed into envelopes with the address stickers already affixed, boxed, and then delivered to the post office. The paper was packaged in 500-sheet reams from Weyerhaeuser, each marked with the slogan "The tree-growing company." The pressmen liked to call it the tree-*killing* company. "Could someone please explain to me what making paper has to do with *growing* trees?" Larry would ask of no one in particular almost every time he popped the band on a fresh box of ten reams.

"Maybe they should call it the tree-*reaming* company," Jason said.

"Tree *reaming*. Heh heh. Yeah. That's good," Larry chuckled. He kept repeating the phrase the entire afternoon. "Tree *reaming*, heh, heh. Yeah. That's good. Tree *reaming*."

Larry saw no harm in letting Jason wrestle with the machine as long as Michael stood watch and stepped in if the deadline got too close. Jason knew a passable sheet might be all right for a subscriber to get once, but he knew he had to improve and improve fast.

But legibility didn't come routinely. Sometimes the ink was too faint or smudged or blackened. Sometimes the thin paper crinkled. The worse part of it all was that Jason felt rushed. The tip sheet was usually dropped off at the shop just in time to burn the plate and slap it on the press, dash off the copies, fold them with the ink still wet and then rush them to the post office eight blocks away just before it closed.

This Friday's run was going perfectly. Jason was the master of the machine. A little more ink, a little less water, a little more speed—Jason and the machine were one. I can do this, Jason thought. I *am* doing this. He cracked open a fresh ream of paper, fanned the sheets and reloaded. He pulled the red rag from his back pocket and touched it lightly to the plate to dab off a glob of ink. The drum suddenly grabbed the rag and pulled it into the press with a loud clatter as Jason instinctively reached down and hit the kill switch. Larry appeared behind Jason, who stood speechless, shaking, staring at the tip of the rag peeking out from between the cylinders. "What happened?" Larry asked.

"Nothing," Michael replied, as he rotated the drum by hand to free it. "The rag got caught. That's all."

"You'd better let Michael finish the run, OK?" Larry said, cigarette in hand. "You just lost your rag this time. Lucky you didn't lose a finger." Larry's faded blue screaming eagle tattoo looked more lively than he did.

Jason knew he had fucked up. It was as if, in the instant he had become confident, the rag jumped out of his hand and into the press. "You have to be more careful, man," Michael said. "That's why we all wear short sleeves and no jewelry—nothing that can get stuck in the press. You don't see me wearing my wedding ring, do you? I leave it home every morning. My wife doesn't like it, but she'd like it even less if I got it caught in the press."

Bill, the paper cutter, was nearing retirement and had been cutting paper there before the old man had bought the shop, which was when the old man was still middle-aged. He walked with a constant stoop and squinted his right eye, a habit he had acquired from leaning over a paper cutter for some thirty-odd years and eyeballing the measurements. Later that afternoon, he squinted at Jason and said, "I don't know what you're doing here anyway. If I was your age, I'd move to Hawaii right now. They've got dumps like this everywhere." This was the first time Bill had said anything to Jason that didn't involve paper.

The next morning, Michael said to Jason, "Larry doesn't want you running the press anymore. He said he knew you wouldn't be able to handle it—you looked too spaced out, like you were stoned or something."

"Well, I definitely wasn't stoned. I don't do that stuff."

"Yeah, right. Anyway, it might have been better if you had been stoned," Michael replied, shaking his head. "At least then you'd have an excuse. But seriously, man—you

Accidental Destination

have to keep your wits about you. Ted there on the color press is missing the tips of two fingers down to the first knuckle. Maybe Larry did you a favor."

Jason knew he had a lot to learn—he hadn't even smelled wet ink before he had walked in here. He'd made a bonehead mistake, but he wouldn't let it happen again. He was smarter than the press. He wasn't sure he could say the same for Larry. And yet Larry was running the joint.

"Thanks for at least giving me a shot," Jason said. "I appreciate it."

Jason assiduously practiced his bass and had even picked up a little amp at a yard sale. He saw less and less of Tim and Marshall these days, but when he did, they were still barreling through the same old songs over and over, so Jason used the opportunity to practice his bass. *This* is the machine I need to master, he told himself as he pounded out rudimentary figures while they ran through another twelve-bar blues. I know the songs inside and out already. I can make them more interesting by adding bass.

One evening, Tim appeared at Jason's door with his arm around a pale, overweight girl whose large aureoles peeked through a thin cotton top held up with spaghetti straps. She looked like she was still in high school. The first words out of Tim's mouth were, "Hey, man—Can you let me use your room for like thirty minutes? See . . . I have this . . . I have to . . . and I thought you might be home. I really need this."

Jason knew Tim was practically living with Stella—a nice girl who didn't deserve this—and Tim knew that Jason knew. They locked eyes. Three seconds passed slowly. Jason crunched his toes together and shrugged. "Sure, man. OK. I'll come back in about forty."

"That's cool, bro. I owe you one."

Jason stood in the hallway and thought about walking downstairs and knocking on Sophia's door. She might be home. She might let him in. Who knows what might transpire? He had seen Sophie's eyes light up whenever they passed in the downstairs hall, as if she were waiting for him to make a move. But no, the feeling had to be mutual. He wasn't going to use Sophie the way Susie had used him. That wouldn't be good karma. He wanted The Real Thing, not some fleeting entanglement. There was too much of that going on in the Boarding House already. He tried not to think about what was going on in his own apartment right now.

Jason stepped across the hall and knocked on Dan's door. He could smell the homegrown from out in the hall. "Hey Dan," he yelled. "It's me—Jason—Can I hang with you a few?"

Dan swung the door open with a blank expression, scratching his scraggly beard. "Sure. Come on in." Jefferson Starship's *Red Octopus* was blasting on his console stereo. The contraption was bigger than a color television and it was his pride and joy. The day he got it working, he caught Jason in the hall and practically pulled him into his room. "Check this out," he had said. "I found it on the curb on garbage day. All I had to do was rewire it. I added a twelve-inch speaker I took out of an old TV set someone else threw away. The things people throw away around here. It's un-believable."

Jason had met Dan a month or so earlier when he and someone else were lugging the stereo up the steps to the second floor. They had made it look easy. "Sorry we're block-ing your path. I'm Dan," he had said, extending his right hand while holding up his end of the stereo with the other.

Except for that afternoon when he was excited about his new acquisition, Dan wasn't much of a talker. And he wasn't saying much tonight, either.

He sat back down on the floor and picked up the cigar box he kept his stash of homegrown (all dark green shake) in and began rolling a joint. He could always be counted on to share his pot freely, although you had to smoke a lot of it to get a buzz. Jason picked up the red album cover with gold embossing. Great cover, but shitty music, he thought. They sucked after they stopped being the Airplane, but maybe now's the time to give them another listen.

Dan lit the fat, loosely rolled joint with his brass Zippo lighter. As he handed the doobie to Jason he said, "If the music's too loud, just turn it down to where you like it. I can't tell. I lost a lot of hearing driving a tank in The Nam." That was all he had to say about it. That, and that he had been drafted.

"Lemme see your lighter," Jason said. "This thing ain't lit." Dan tossed it to Jason. The front was inscribed with the words VIET NAM, LAI KHE 70-71 and some sort of patch. The back was inscribed with the words DEATH IS MY BUSINESS AND BUSINESS HAS BEEN GOOD, in all caps.

Dan stared at Jason, but he seemed to be looking through him. He sat cross-legged in his jungle boots. Jason had never seen him without them, even when he practiced his karate kata every morning in the backyard.

"Hey man, it's 10 'o clock at night," Jason said. "Why don't you take off your boots and stay awhile?"

"You've got to be ready at all times," Dan replied. "The enemy won't wait for you to put on your shoes." He said it in a soft-spoken manner, as if he were revisiting a memory, rather than imparting information.

Jason would sometimes watch him practice from his window as he drank his morning coffee. The guy was lightning fast. He knew what he was doing. He had technique.

Dan sometimes practiced shirtless, his back and torso displaying a mass of chemical burns and scars, rumored to be from Agent Orange. Sitting here on the floor, he looked so gentle, so fragile, that if he ever did trip one of the landmines in his brain, he would be the only one injured by the implosion.

Jason thought back to when he had walked into the draft board to register. He wore hand-patched blue jeans and his hair, parted in the middle, hung well past his shoulders. A crew-cutted man in dress uniform with sharp creases all over it asked him a number of questions. When asked his occupation, Jason had replied, "I'm a folksinger."

The soldier moved close enough to Jason for him to smell his breath and raised his voice. "No, *really*—what *are* you?" His crew-cutted buddies gathered around, spines erect, muscles taut, all eyes on Jason. His mouth got dry.

Coming here had been a calculated risk, a compromise

to silence his parents' incessant cajoling and pleading to "at least register." Maybe his number wouldn't come up and he wouldn't have to refuse induction. Most of his friends were scared—scared shitless—of being drafted and shipped off to Vietnam. Scared of dying face down in the jungle mud—or maybe even worse—being captured and tortured by those faceless, gibbering Commie gooks.

But Jason wasn't scared—not of that. He was terrified of the Army mentality. He could never be molded into a soldier. He'd never even held a gun and had no desire to. And the way these guys were acting? Imagine if they got him on an Army base. No way he was going to be inducted. It was a free country. It was his choice. Everyone had a choice, didn't they?

Dan had grown up in a small town in southern Oregon and had probably accepted his draft notice with equanimity, without question—thinking he'd do his duty and return home to his job in the mill.

But those bullies at the draft board had to have had way more choices than Dan ever had. Or maybe they didn't. Maybe they came from a long line of My-Country-Right-or-Wrong-Love-It-or-Leave-It types and had been brainwashed long before they had enlisted. Maybe they had signed up to escape poverty and were now cramming fodder into the belly of The War Machine to keep their own pale asses out of harm's way. Maybe they had been drafted too. You never know.

But Jason knew *he* shouldn't be here registering—even that concession went against everything he knew he was, and standing up to these balls-to-the-wall GI Joes was his only chance at salvaging whatever he had left of his dignity.

"*Really*, I'm a folksinger," he said. After repeating himself several times, the soldier wrote down "folksinger" as Jason's occupation.

Jason passed the joint back to Dan, but held on to the Zippo, turning it over in his hand. He had never heard back from the Army. Maybe his number hadn't come up. Maybe the war had wound down and they didn't need him. Or maybe—just maybe—Jason liked to think, they had passed

Accidental Destination

him over because they knew he'd throw a left-handed monkey wrench into their ranks. In any event, he had never received a draft card.

But Dan *had* gone to Vietnam. And he didn't look or act like any of those assholes at the draft board. Stoned or not, Jason thought, Dan's body has returned, but Dan hasn't. And now we're living across from each other in this ramshackle boarding house. It's OK for me, but for *him*? His country—*my* country—*our* country—used him up and threw him away like human garbage. Even I feel uncomfortable around him. I don't know what it is, but something about him makes me nervous.

Jason stared at the bumper sticker on the wall behind Dan: "Join the Army, Travel to Foreign Lands, Meet Exotic Peoples—and Kill Them!" How many people had Dan killed? Jason didn't want to know.

When Side 2 finished, Jason stood up. "Thanks, man. I gotta get back. You like Starship?"

"I guess so. I don't know. I found it in the free box at the market up the street."

"Great cover," Jason said. But the band sucks, he thought. And Tim sucks. And I suck for letting him use my room. But what could I do? I couldn't say no. He's the oldest friend I've got here. My connection to this place. That fat fuck's gotta be legal, but Tim's got a great girl. He doesn't deserve her. It's only a matter of time before she dumps his cheating ass.

Jason stood up. "OK man, see ya later," he said.

Dan remained seated, staring at the album cover, rocking it back and forth, watching the light reflect off the gold embossing. Jason opened the door and walked out. When he shut it behind him, it locked automatically. He knocked lightly on his own door and Tim opened it. The girl had both arms around Tim's waist, resting her head on his shoulder as if she were glued to him. Her face was flushed red and her stomach protruded from the bottom of her tank top. They were standing on a blanket in his kitchen.

"Tim—What the fuck?!" The words slipped out before Jason could stop them.

Tim took a swig of the quart of beer he had brought with him and answered easily: "I met her tonight outside the bus station. She said she wanted to get pregnant and I told her I'd give it my best shot. So that's what I did." He cocked his head to the side. "Now we gotta go." He pulled the girl's top down to cover her belly fat and grabbed her hand. "I'll catch you later, OK? Thanks again, bro."

Jason didn't know whether the work at Lasting Impression or his coworkers were becoming more tedious, but after the press incident, he saw no future there and just went through the motions to collect his paycheck every Friday at noon. *I thought learning to run a press would turn things around for me—but I can't even do that,* he thought.

That Friday, the paychecks were late. Shortly after noon, Larry walked out of the old man's office and into the pressroom. "I'm sorry," he said, "but the checks are going to be a couple of hours late today. I'm not sure what the deal is."

"Someone's getting fired," Michael said to no one in particular.

"Yeah, probably," the man running the color press said. "The old man always does this when he fires someone."

Larry raised an eyebrow and shrugged.

"Maybe the checks really are late," Jason said to Bill at 3 p.m.

"No—I know the old man. He likes to squeeze every last hour he can out of his workers. If I had to guess, you're the one getting the ax. He never liked you."

"Shit. I know," Jason said. At 4:30, Larry walked into the pressroom and began handing out checks. He handed Jason an envelope and moved on. *Good. Maybe I'm spared,* he thought. Jason opened the envelope and, along with his check, found a pink slip of paper that said his employment was terminated effective 5 p.m. today. *So this is a pink slip,* he thought. *I thought it was just a saying. I can't believe that cocksucker couldn't tell me in person.*

The pink slip was hard for anyone to miss, especially for someone who could eyeball measurements down to 1/64 of an inch. "I'm sorry Jason," Bill said. "The old crank always does it like that. He doesn't have the balls to fire someone to his face."

The pressmen all made fun of Bill, but he was OK. Bill extended his hand. He was standing up straight and wasn't squinting. "Nice working with you. You're a good kid. You don't need this place."

Jason walked back to the drill press and began sweeping up after the job he had just finished. Larry walked up behind him. "Don't worry about that. You can just go now if you want."

Jason looked up and glanced over the pressroom. Everyone appeared busy at their jobs, oblivious to him. "OK," he said, as he turned and walked out the back door without a word to anyone else.

Jason felt light, as if a weight had been lifted. I don't need this dead end job—these guys are all assholes or losers, he thought. Larry's the squirreliest of them all—Mr. Dishonor Before Death. Fuck him. And Michael's a nice guy, but he can barely keep up with the payments on his trailer and now his wife is pregnant again. He's not going anywhere. None of them are going anywhere. Bill was the only one decent enough to say goodbye. And I don't want to wake up twenty years from now and be him. No, six months here was plenty.

"It's unemployment tiiime a-gaaaain," he sang as he raised his hands to the late afternoon sky and let the sheets of cool rain pour over him.

13

THESE ARE THE PEOPLE
WHO MAKE THE BLUES

At three in the afternoon, the Caribou Bar was nearly deserted. With the houselights on low and the double doors in back propped open, the bar looked much less appealing to Jason than it had during his nocturnal visits. A mop and bucket resting against the wall stunk of ammonia, but it was not enough to overpower the stench of stale beer. A morbidly obese man in an oversized T-shirt printed like a tuxedo with a nametag affixed that read "Hello I'm: Sexy and I Know It" sipped a draft beer behind the bar.

Even at night the place was a real dive, but in the empty light of day, Jason wondered why anyone would willingly come here. The felt on the two pool tables in the center of the room was scratched and worn; the Tumwater beer sign—with its plastic water cascading down plastic mountains—was filthy with dust. Water spots dotted the acoustic tiles on the ceiling, and the exposed pipes, rather than looking ruggedly industrial, looked like they might swing loose at any moment.

Jason set his bass case down near the small plywood platform shoved against the wall near the double doors. A woman walked in carrying a panel of stage lights. She saw Jason, quickened her pace and nodded. "Hey—Jason, right?

I caught you a couple of weeks ago at the Saturday Market backing up Slim. He don't need to be playin' in a joint like this. But I do. Hey—I'm Laredo."

She looked and talked tough.

"Laredo? Laredo what?"

"Laredo nothin'. Just Laredo."

"That's a cool name. Why Laredo?"

"It's where I'm from. It's just a name. There's some people out there who want me found, but I don't want to be found, you dig?"

"You don't sound like you're from Texas."

"I'm from all over. Look—ya want my life story or ya wanna play bass?"

Her unpolished boots looked stirrup scuffed. She wore a denim Carhartt shirt and a belt adorned with hand-hammered silver medallions. She looked like she could rope and ride and, except for the long silk scarf draped over her neck, she looked like she was ready to.

Jason could almost smell the prairie wind and buffalo dung. "It doesn't matter to me where you're from."

"The way this works is that you're the bass player. Mitch over there is on drums." She cocked her head sideways toward a human skeleton in Wranglers and a rumpled pocket-T sitting at one of the small rectangular tables. His hair and beard were white.

"I'll emcee," Laredo continued. "Sometimes I'll play with whoever gets up there, sometimes I won't. It depends. We'll split the cover three ways and you probably won't have to worry about buying your own beer."

"Hey, I just want to get out there and make something happen," Jason replied.

"You hung in there great with Slim last whenever it was. Remember—there'll probably be a bunch of yahoos up here tonight crowding the stage and breathing our air—Just keep it in the pocket and hang in the background. This could be a regular thing or not. It depends on how it goes tonight. A reporter from the college paper is supposed to do a write-up on the show, so that'll give us some publicity." She snorted. "I don't know why that Nike and Vuarnet crowd is interested in this, but whatever. Let's run through a tune or two as a soundcheck." She strapped on her guitar, as beat up an old Strat as Jason had ever seen. "Hey Mitch," she yelled—"Time to lock 'n' load."

"Rock 'n' roll," the man at the table replied as he stood up in slow motion and positioned himself on the stool behind the drum kit. He set his pint bottle of Ranier on the floor tom, picked up his sticks and tapped the hi-hat and snare. "Mitchell, this is Jason. Jason, this is Mitchell," Laredo said. "Mitch did some sessions in Muscle Shoals but he didn't get credit on the albums. And Jason just did an outdoor gig with Slim here in Emerald."

"I didn't know Slim was so well known," Jason said.

"He's not," Laredo replied. "Just us blues guys know about him. I guess he had enough of that Cleveland scene."

"He *ain't* nothing," Mitchell said. "Ah *mean*, he's *something*. He shared the stage with Muddy and Jimmy Reed. Suh muthurs, too"—*Some others, too*—"John Lee Hooker maybe, Ah thank"—*I think*—"Anyway, it's good to know ya," he said, saluting with a drumstick.

Before Jason could even plug in to tune up, Laredo grabbed the microphone, clutched the stand and belted out what at first sounded like nonsense syllables: "Whoa . . . Whoaa . . . Whoaaa . . . baay . . . aaay beee . . ." The only two customers in the joint looked up from their pool game and Mr. I'm-Sexy-and-I-Know-It moved out from behind the bar and stood a little closer to the stage. Laredo acted as if she were singing to a packed house. She turned her head toward Jason. "OK. This is in Bb," she said, giving her guitar a single strum that rang out as forcefully as her voice.

Jason struggled to find a Bb. He did and then tried to hit one of the simple blues figures he knew. He hung mostly on the root note on the downbeats and tried not to hit any bum notes while trying to sync in to the beat of the kick drum. This guy Mitchell was solid.

Laredo stopped abruptly in the middle of the song and said, "Yeah—OK. Something like that. That's cool. We're good. I'll see you guys tonight, all right?" Mitchell took a swig of his now-warm Ranier, raised the bottle in the same manner that No-Booze Bob had raised his coffee cup, and winked at Jason. "Good job, man."

Who *are* these guys? Jason wondered. And how did I get mixed up with them? This could be the steady gig I've been looking for. I know I still kinda suck on bass, but if I show up and play it cool, who knows? I might even be able to get Laredo to sing a couple of my blues numbers.

Jason spent most of that afternoon with a bass instruction book, reviewing a few common blues riffs that used no open strings. That way he could easily transpose them to any key. He made sure he could find the Bb with his eyes closed. These riffs are total clichés, he thought, but I need to know them backwards and forwards. I can't be fumbling around in the middle of a song. I just gotta get through tonight. I'll be fine if I can just get through tonight.

That night, Jason arrived a little before nine, bass in one hand, amplifier in the other. The lights were low and the bar was still half empty. "That little amp ain't gonna to cut it here," were the first words out of Laredo's mouth, followed by a stream of cigarette smoke. "You can plug into the PA tonight, but if we keep this up, you're gonna need something bigger."

"Hey, I'm a bluesman. I'm lucky to even have a bass. When Slim came to town, all he had was that beat-up old Yamaha acoustic. He had to scrounge up an electric for that Saturday Market gig . . . but yeah, I hear ya."

Laredo threw her half-smoked cigarette to the concrete floor and stamped it out with her boot. "All right. We might as well get started," she said as she checked the sign-up sheet. "Four names so far. Not bad. There'll be more later on. We'll do a few numbers first and then I'll call up the first name and we'll play this by ear."

"I'm on bass," Jason said, trying to sound nonchalant. He had never played an unrehearsed gig like this, and Laredo was so tough and confident, and Mitchell was so smooth, he was almost invisible. Mitch later told him that Laredo was happy to have *anyone* on bass with such short notice, especially someone essentially playing for free, and that he was just happy to get away from the wife and kids and pound the skins for a few hours. But right here, right now, Jason was sweating it. He hoped he could hear his bass through the PA. He hoped he wouldn't fuck up. He hoped he was in tune with Laredo. He had tuned to a pitchpipe earlier in the afternoon, but he didn't know about Laredo. He suspected that she was not that meticulous about being at concert pitch.

Mitchell was already onstage, striking the hi-hat and bass drum with his feet and expertly twirling a drumstick before grabbing it and coming down on the snare with a sharp staccato. He kept repeating this action, and Jason realized he was establishing a groove. Jason stepped onstage and rested his arms on top of his bass. The stage seemed even smaller than it had during the afternoon soundcheck. Laredo turned to Jason, and strummed an A chord, almost bumping him with the head of her guitar. "Are we in tune?" she asked. Miraculously, they were. "All right. Let's do this one in A this time," she said. Jason wiggled his toes.

Laredo strummed an A chord and let it ring. "Good evening ladies and gentlemen and thanks for coming out to the Caribou tonight for our first ever blues open-mic night." She worked the A chord until Jason came in behind her.

She started in with the same "Whoa . . . Whoaa . . . Whoaaa . . ." like she had done at the afternoon soundcheck. As her voice rang out though the PA system, the room got quiet and every eye turned to the stage. She dropped into a standard blues number, the crowd resumed their conversations and the clack of pool balls once again punctuated the air.

Laredo played two more songs and introduced the first guest performer. He had hair to the middle of his back and round wire-rimmed glasses. He plugged in a red Gibson SG and began playing the opening chords to the Allman Brothers' "Melissa." It was bluesy, without really being the blues. Jason knew this one because he had played it ad nauseam with Tim and Marshall. From there, the guy launched into a standard twelve-bar blues progression and began singing something about having the blues every day and every night.

Laredo was a pro. She knew how to share a small stage. This guy didn't. Jason felt more cramped than ever. He kept his head down, his ear to the snare and bass drum and his mind on the music. Most of the performers played in the keys of E or A, so he didn't have to fumble around for the notes.

Performers came and went. They all blended together as the night wore on. I don't know why I was so nervous about this, Jason thought. I may suck, but most of these guys suck worse. I just gotta keep at it, that's all.

Jason swigged beers between songs but didn't feel the least bit drunk. Mitch nonchalantly sipped his beer, even in the middle of songs. Jason figured it was his way of showing off, of reviewing the performers, because if Mitch liked a guy he'd appear to give it his all, furrowing his brow in mock concentration and puckering his lips, even though Jason knew Mitch could produce any of these beats with one hand.

The beer and blues kept flowing, and Jason developed blisters on the fingers of both of his hands. His fingers and shoulders ached. He hadn't expected to get so tired. It was like running a high-decibel marathon. But he kept going, just trying to make it through. *This is work*, he thought, as he retuned his bass between songs.

People, performers mostly, bought him more beers than he could drink. He lined them up unopened, telling anyone who offered to buy him one, "Look how many I still have. You don't need to buy me another." Yet, they did.

Toward the end of the night, as the crowd thinned out, a pixie with raspberry hair slipped into the bar and sat down at an empty table near the stage without ordering a drink. Jason spotted her immediately—Sophie, from the Boarding House. He had never noticed how cute she was, in a chipmunk kind of way. How many times had he passed her in the hall and not given her a second thought?

As Jason slogged through another interminable twelve-bar blues, he began picking the open E and A strings with his right hand. He grabbed an unopened beer with his left, walked offstage and set it down on Sophie's table. "Hey, Sophie with the raspberry hair," he sang, and then he began playing again with both hands.

"Thanks, Jay," she replied. Hearing himself being called Jay almost made him skip a beat. But he didn't. He kept repeating the root note and the fifth, half listening to the band, staring directly into Sophie's eyes. "I wish I could sit here with you longer, but I can't make it look this easy. I have to put on a show. I'll talk to you later, OK? Don't go anywhere." He walked slowly back to the stage, feeling pretty good about such a slick maneuver.

She's come to see me, he thought. Something about her—maybe it was those green eyes or the way her hair cascaded over her forehead—but whatever it was made him want to show off. He exaggerated his body movements and motioned rhythmically with his bass. She smiled, never taking her eyes off him. He stepped offstage again, still playing, and sat down next to her. "I see you've changed your hair color again," he said, bringing his mouth close to her ear, trying to be heard over the music and bar noise. She shook her head up and down. He sat there, still playing, for maybe thirty seconds, and then stood up and walked backwards toward the stage, bobbing his head to the music, not missing a beat. Mitchell pointed a drumstick at him and winked.

When the last performer had finished, Laredo said, "Thanks everybody for coming out to the first Caribou blues jam. We'll be back here again in two weeks. We'll see y'all then." She launched into one last song, a showcase number, giving it all she had. She even put a big musical ending on it, conducting with her guitar neck. The audience began hooting and applauding before the band had even slowed down. After the last notes rang out, the three musicians bowed in unison. Laredo, out of breath, waved and shouted, "Thanks again, everybody."

"Great job, guys," she said to Jason and Mitch as she patted the sweat off her face with her scarf. "Maybe I'll catch up with you before the next show, but in any case, I'll see you back here for that. Maybe we should come up with a name for the band. Think about it. Jason—Now go see to that girl of yours over there. You don't want to leave her sitting all alone like that."

Jason walked over and sat down at Sophie's table. He looked into her eyes. "Hi," he said.

"Hi," she replied. Neither spoke for what, to Jason, seemed like minutes. Glasses clinked, people shouted to each other across the room, a man stumbled into a table full of empties, and the neon signs in the windows buzzed. But Jason heard none of it as he watched Sophie roll her empty beer bottle gently between her palms.

"Listen," he said, "It's getting late. Can I give you a ride home?"

"No. I drove here."

"Well then, let me walk you to your car."

"Sure. Why not."

Jason stood up, packed away his bass, and touched Sophie on the back. "All set. Let's go." He turned to Laredo and Mitchell who were still packing up their gear. "So long, guys," he yelled. "Thanks. I'll see you later."

Laredo nodded. Mitchell didn't seem to have heard him.

When they reached her car, a faded maroon Datsun that didn't look like it had many more miles in it, Jason moved his tongue back and forth inside his mouth to relieve the dryness and asked, "Would you like to meet up when we get back to the house?"

"I would, I really would," she said, wrapping her arms around his neck. "I would, but no. I can't. There was a time when I would have, but now I need more than a drunken slam, bam, thank you ma'am—You know what *that* is, don't you?"

Car doors slammed and engines rumbled around them. Neon from the bar signs reflected on the parking lot gravel. A man tried to steady a woman who kept repeating, "I shaw you schtaring at that schlut. I shaw you."

Sophia swiveled her head to take in the scene, then pulled Jason to her and kissed him. "Ask me out on a regular date sometime, and we'll see what happens," she whispered.

She released him, quickly got into her car and eased it out of its parking space. Jason watched her tail lights disappear over the railroad tracks. He inhaled slowly and clasped his hand to his heart. He still felt the electricity from her kiss. I should have kissed her a long time ago, he thought.

It wasn't until Jason got home that he realized Laredo hadn't given him his cut of the cover charge.

14

VIEW FROM
THE PONDEROSA

It wasn't yet light when Jason heard a gentle tapping on his door. "Jason, it's me. Let me in," Sophie whispered. He barely heard the whisper, but, half asleep, he opened the door without checking to see who it was. She was wearing a faded terrycloth robe and slipped wordlessly into the room. She opened the robe and, arching her shoulders back, dropped it to the floor, revealing a thin, green negligee. "Oh, Jay," she said. "I'm sorry I kept you waiting. I was just teasing about a real date. You can take me out for breakfast later. Come here, lay down beside me now and hold me. We've both waited long enough." She slid under the covers and Jason followed her. He wrapped her in his arms as she had asked. She smelled fresh, maybe of talcum. Certainly not of beer and bar smoke. This girl was all right.

From that morning on, they hung out every day. Jason liked her. He liked her hair, dark and shaggy after she washed the water-based dyes out of it. He liked the way she cradled her coffee cup, nearly concealing it in her long, thin fingers. He liked the racks and racks of costumes that filled every room of her downstairs apartment, except the kitchen. And she liked him too, although she couldn't say why. "I don't know *why*. I just *do*. Isn't that enough?" she'd reply whenever Jason asked.

But this wasn't going to be a forever thing. Jason thought so and he thought that Sophia thought so too. Nothing lasted in this vagabond town. Susie was gone. No great loss there. Flute Girl was—well, he didn't know where she was or whether she was dead or alive. Whenever he thought of her—which he tried not to—he didn't know which Flute Girl would appear to him, the joyful one at the Saturday Market, twirling and laughing at this life on Earth, or the comatose one lying motionless in that hospital bed. And Sophie would be graduating this June. That gave them just—he didn't want to do the math.

The blues jams continued, but the unemployment-check clock kept winding down with each passing week. The problem of money would soon present itself again. Jason sat at the kitchen table and stared at the bare plum tree, baffled. He had no answer. I gotta do something, he thought. But what? Earning a living playing music would be ideal, but the closest I've come to that is splitting the cover charge at the blues jam every two weeks. Slim is doing it, but he's barely hanging on to that studio apartment of his.

And little wonder. We're all living in what amounts to a small town surrounded by a wilderness of trees. And more trees. And rain. Pounding rain. Pouring rain. Sheets of rain. Blankets of rain. Vertical rain. Oblique rain. Relentless rain. Blowing rain. Walls of rain. Curtains of rain. Buckets of rain. Boxes of rain. Distant rain. Intermittent rain. Soaking rain. Light rain. Drizzling rain. Hard rain. Driving rain. Drenching rain. Diagonal rain. Sizzling rain. Sprinkling rain. Hissing rain. Jackhammer rain. Pitter-patter rain. Threatening rain. Gentle rain. Drops of rain. Rain in the forecast. Rainy days and rainy nights. Incessant rain. Cold rain. Sleeting rain. Freezing rain. Winter rain. Spring rain. Summer rain. Falling Rain. Early morning rain. Rain. And more rain. And trees. And more trees.

Maybe I could plant trees, Jason thought. He had seen those ragged, dirt-encrusted guys, reeking of mud, pine sap and an aggregate of human secretions, congregating at the Anthill and he wondered what it would be like roughing it in a communal tent for a week or more on a clearcut mountainside, whomping a hoedad into the ground with a bag of seedlings slung over his shoulder, breathing in the mountain air and—planting trees. Lots of guys were doing it. Maybe Hoedad Hank from CETA had a point. It *was* a holy profession. Even if I only last a single day and plant a couple of hundred trees—or even a couple—that would mean something, he thought, recalling the parks in Newark, which had fewer trees than downtown Emerald.

Jason headed to the Anthill to find Vodka. Vodka could get him on a crew. But Vodka wasn't expected back for a few weeks. He was somewhere in California, working on a fire crew.

So Jason poked his head into Stu's room. Stu never locked his door, but he didn't have anything of value in there either—that is, nothing anyone in the Anthill would consider valuable. When Jason was renting the room across the hall, Stu didn't mind if he came in and hung out when he wasn't there. He liked Jason and liked having someone keep an eye on his room.

Stu was an anomaly at the Anthill—he studied astrophysics at the university (although he just called it *physics*) and usually spent at least three nights a week gathering data at the Green Mountain Observatory. Once, when Jason had asked, he said that his full name was Stuart, but that sounded too nerdy and only his mother called him that, so please keep calling him Stu. And while Stu didn't look like the stereotypical nerd with a pocket protector and tape holding together a pair of horn-rimmed glasses, with his thin frame, his Oxford shirts with crisscross line patterns and close-cropped hair, he didn't look much like the average Anthillian either. For him, the Anthill was the perfect crash pad.

Jason stepped into the room, sat down and picked up an elementary calculus textbook. He gathered that somehow math was being used to determine the volume of irregularly shaped three-dimensional objects, but the equations were gibberish and the text didn't help him disambiguate them. He closed it and picked up another: *The Physics of Sound.*

This one was filled with drawings of sine waves and graphs representing the properties of sound vibrations, invisible to the eye. The text made little sense to him, but he read through it slowly, trying to grasp it. He knew this book could be the key to unlocking the mysteries of sound. There is more to music than meets the ear, he thought.

Stu had entered the room so quietly that Jason didn't hear him. "Oh yes, right. *The Physics of Sound.* That's a good introductory text." He spoke nonchalantly, as if he'd seen Jason yesterday, rather than more than a year ago. "I just came in here to grab a change of clothes and a shower. I'm headed out to The Ponderosa to check on a few things. It's the middle of winter, so work can go on for almost twelve hours, but I don't need that much time. If you're not doing anything and you want to, you can come along."

The Ponderosa was home to a telescope (two, if you want to be entirely accurate and count the smaller one) atop a mountain some 100 miles west of Emerald and eight miles south of the middle of nowhere. Its official name was The Green Mountain Observatory, but it had long ago been nicknamed The Ponderosa because the mountain was covered with huge ponderosa pines. According to Stu, the telescope was *significant* as far as North American telescopes went, and some important research was being done on black hole binaries by the university, where professors crunched numbers and published the results obtained from their students' raw data.

Jason thought it would be cool to look at stars from on top of a mountain. Besides, he had a couple of hits of acid that would be perfect for enhancing the experience. "Sounds good," he said.

"OK, great. Meet me back here in four hours. That way it'll be good and dark by the time we get there. And be sure to bring the warmest coat you've got. It'll get colder than you think. Maybe even below zero."

Stu was an Oregon native and, like many such natives, he was outdoorsy—not in a gung-ho way—but seamlessly, effortlessly. It was part of who he was and he didn't really think about it. "There's almost a full moon, so there'll be

Accidental Destination

plenty of light from the sky. Maybe we could even do a little hiking while we're at it," he added.

Before Jason had come to Emerald, the outdoors was where he went when he crossed the street to get from one apartment to another. New Jersey is a land of interiors—Oregon, a land of exteriors. No wonder Stu was comfortable in this little room. It was a place to crash, an address on an envelope, a place to call home. It was all he needed. But Jason needed more than this. He needed a safe harbor, someplace he could call his own, a home he could always go home to. Part of him imagined it lined with bookshelves built into the walls, a high-end stereo system, a down quilt for those wet winter nights, a set of chef's grade cooking knives . . . Things he had abandoned for this journey Westward, things he had never had, things he knew he could live without, things that rust and wear out, things that break and beg to be replaced, things he didn't know why he had wanted in the first place. He wanted to embrace thingless-ness—and he had tried—he had left New Jersey and come to Emerald with just a backpack and his guitar. But he was still caught between the borders of these two worlds, in a blended territory of desire for both, a product of constraints and inherited beliefs that had become second nature, imbedded and calcified, and were hard to separate from the Jason he had been, the Jason he was slowly becoming, and the Jason he wanted to be.

"I'll wear my hiking boots, just in case," Jason replied.

Four hours later, he was sitting in a bucket seat in Stu's Pontiac coupe (with dual overhead cams) heading for the Ponderosa. Jason didn't know what a cam was, much less the value of them being *dual* and *overhead*, but Stu always referred to his car that way, possibly because he was constantly reminded of this feature due to the upkeep it required. But far from it being a burden, Stu relished keeping his machine in top shape. "I just changed the oil this morning," he said. "Unlike humans, machines can't repair themselves."

The divided highway out of town turned into a two-lane and, as they ascended the mountain slopes, snow suddenly began to fall and stick to the ground. Jason could see the large, wet flakes illuminated in the car's headlights. They passed a sign reading *Snow Chains Required Through Green Mountain Pass*. Stu pulled over, grabbed his chains from the trunk and began attaching them to the rear tires. "The snow's not so bad yet," he said. "But it'll get heavier as we go on. The curves and inclines will be particularly treacherous . . . Yes, right. Famous last words." Stu laughed at his own joke and reached into the car to shut off the headlights. "Look around you . . . See—no manmade light whatsoever."

Jason looked up at the sky drenched with stars. There are so many stars, it looks like it's about to rain stars, he thought. He didn't want to say it aloud. It'd sound too silly. "There are more stars here than anywhere I've ever been," he said.

"Yes, right. Actually there are the same number everywhere. You can just see them better out here."

"And I bet they're even here during the daytime, right?"

"You've got it," Stu replied.

Several miles ahead, a building with a lighted sign that read *Liminac Store* came into view. Stu pulled off the road. "Let's gas up and pick up some provisions," he said. "You've got to check this place out—there's not another store or gas station for thirty miles in any direction. This is actually the *town* of Liminac. It's got to be the smallest town in the state. The loneliest dot on the Oregon map. It's just Nestor and his family living here."

A man walked out of the store clutching a Dr. Pepper to his chest with his right arm, and Stu yelled to him, "Fill 'er up with high-test." When he got closer, Jason noticed that he was missing his right hand. He also noticed that the price of gas was much higher than in town. You'd have to be pretty desperate to gas up here, he thought.

"C'mon," Stu said. "Check out the store. It's even got a post office." To Jason, the place looked cramped and smelled stuffy. Racks of pepperoni, leather gloves, pliers, rolls of barbed wire, a glass jar filled with pretzel rods, bottles of soda, cans of stew, oil, Sterno, batteries—you name it—

were scattered throughout the large room in an apparently random fashion. There was even an antelope head mounted on the wall. An old man sat in the shadows on a wooden rocker in the back of the store, watching a snowy black-and-white television with rabbit ears. "Hi Nestor," Stu said. "Any mail for us?"

"Nope. Boys got it earlier."

"Yes, right. You'd better give me a six pack of Ranier then." Stu grabbed a package of chips, some jerky and a couple of cans of soup. He turned to Jason. "This should do us."

All right—beer, Jason thought, but it's not gonna be enough. He knew Stu wasn't much of a beer drinker, but even so.

Stu and Jason pulled out of the Liminac Store (and simultaneously, the town of Liminac) and in less than a minute they were heading up the gravel road to the telescope. The clank of the snow chains softened to a gentle crunch. "Pretty handy to have a store right here," Jason said.

"It's further up the road than you think. We've still got another eight miles to go."

"Pretty dour guy," Jason said.

"Yeah. But he loves that place. Catch him at the right time, when he's sipping his Ole Loudmouth, and he might offer you a snort and chew your ear off. He won't live any place else. He loves the stars here—amazing so far from the city lights in this high desert. You'll get a better sense of how isolated this place is in the morning."

As Jason entered the observatory's common room, he saw two men pouring over yards of computer printouts. They looked up at Stu in unison, and the one smoking a corncob pipe said, "Hey, Stuart. We didn't expect you tonight. Did you bring us any beer?"

"You bet," Stu replied, pulling out the six-pack. "Nestor mentioned you were here, so I grabbed this for you." Stu turned to Jason. "That's the first thing anyone up here asks. 'Did you bring any beer?' But no one ever does. So this time I surprised them and did."

The two men droned on. "Add a second modulator. That would chop out the second-order effects."

"But that will reduce the effective chopping frequency to a few hundred hertz," the one with the corncob said as he struck a match and held it to his pipe, waving the match in the air and exhaling a cloud of tobacco smoke.

"Yes, right. But you would still be well above the electronic and the sky noise too," Stu said, handing them each a beer.

So *this* is what *Stuart* is into, Jason thought.

"The 'scope is already in use tonight," Stu said, turning back to Jason. "So I can't let you look through it. Let's just hang out in the quarters and go hiking tomorrow morning."

Stu and Jason threw their packs on the floor of what to Jason looked like a rustic little cabin. Stu turned up the electric baseboard heat. "This place really needs a wood-stove," he said, "but for various reasons we'll never get one." He saw Jason rummaging for a clean cup in the cabinet above a sink filled with unwashed dishes. "Yes, right. We've got to make the 2,000 gallons in the cistern last until spring, but some people go overboard with water conservation. Anyway, make sure you shut the faucet off the second you're done with it and don't flush the toilet unless you absolutely have to. There's no way to know how much water is left. If we run out before spring, that's it."

Jason and Stu settled in. There was little, if anything, to do. Nothing to read except a few ten-year-old *Playboy* magazines. Jason picked one up and idly thumbed through it. Fashion and photographic techniques may have changed, but girls were still girls and these girls still looked good. It occurred to him that in real life these models were now ten years older than their photos and they would still look good.

Jason liked *Playboy*. Of course there were the photos, but he also found it witty, especially the Playboy Advisor and the Playboy Dictionary. "Hey, Stu—" he asked, "Do you know what 'parlay' means?"

"Yeah—an average one. I must have read that ten times already. Check out these blackout blinds. We work all night and if we catch a glimpse of the sun, there's no getting any sleep. There's not much for two guys to do here until morning. But listen—We're far from the streetlights and traffic . . . It's really quiet out here. Listen . . . I mean *really* listen. What do you hear?"

Jason closed his eyes. He heard a bird squawk in the distance. Then a tittering, a sort of rustling . . . an intermittent sibilance. That had to be the wind. And some branches slapping against branches . . . a thud. "Was that a clump of snow hitting the ground?"

"Yes . . . right," Stu replied. "What else could it be? The silence allows you to hear the most amazing things." Stu was still wearing his jacket, and he pulled a baggie and a deer antler pipe out of one of its pockets. "Looks like we're down for the night. We could always smoke some pot."

"Sure," Jason replied. "But would you care for something a little more . . . *subversive*?"

"What do you mean?"

"I've got two hits of acid. Orange barrel . . . some really good stuff. I've been hanging on to it for a special occasion and up here in the mountains might be it. We could drop it now, peak and be all mellow for a walk outside when it starts getting light."

"I don't know. I've never done acid before."

"Well, you've explored outer space. Here's a chance to explore inner space," Jason replied.

"What's it like?"

"It's impossible to describe. I imagine it's different for everyone. Whatever you've heard about it is either a lie or, at best, a half truth. Words can't communicate it. It brings out what's already inside of you. It's a catalyst. Monks take it and see God. Hell's Angels take it and beat people up with pool cues. It helps you see the world as it is—but from your own perspective. You always come down and see the world differently. Sometimes it's as simple as just knowing it's time to clean your room."

"Yes . . . right. But I don't want to have a bad trip and freak out."

"I've never had a bad trip. In fact, I've never known anyone to have a truly bad trip. I'm not saying *you* won't have one, but whatever happens, remember that it's just the drug and it won't last. The trick is to hold on to the beauty and the insights. When you're tripping, you think you'll remember, but it's like a beautiful dream. You wake up and feel it receding. You try to hold on to it, but it slips through your consciousness. It's like you're dreaming you're awake, and then you wake up and wonder where the you who was awake in your dream went."

Jason patted the shirt pocket that contained the acid. "I don't think someone like you has anything to worry about. Have you ever done mushrooms?"

"Once."

"Well it's kinda like 'shrooms, only not really. It's a lot more intense."

"I hear that your senses get all mixed up and you hear colors and see sounds."

"I've heard that too," Jason replied, "but it's never happened to me. I wish. It's more like the whole world slows down and you slow down with it and see things that you know you should be able to see anyway. Like the wood on this wall. The beauty of the grain and how this knot fits in perfectly with the design. How it used to be part of a tree and how in a way it still is. You don't need drugs to see that, but I wonder if I would have seen it if I had never done them. An expanded mind never fully returns to its former self."

Jason had never tried to explain any of this before. He crunched his toes together as he thought of the ludicrous depictions in anti-drug propaganda, and the difficulty of communicating any experience—much less this particular one.

The choked inadequacy of words is, at best, the creaking of muddy wagon wheels or the whinny of a bucking bronco that leaves its rider splayed and aching in the dirt, while his mind struggles to grasp the heavens it's glimpsed.

"It's a tool," Jason continued. "Nothing more. It helps you pull back the veil. I think this would be a great place to take it, in the midst of all this nature. It's up to you. I'm just offering. If you don't want to do it, that's cool. You don't have to. It's like Ken Kesey said: 'You're either on the bus or you're off the bus.'"

"Yes . . . right. OK, then—let's catch the bus." Stu smiled like a mischievous boy agreeing to cut school.

Jason pulled the envelope with the two orange pellets out of his pocket. "Think of LSD as a key to unlocking your brain. You're gonna find it's much bigger than you thought it was. Like the universe. Whatever happens, just remember that ultimately it's your brain—not the drug—that's doing it." Jason handed a tab to Stu.

"Down the hatch," Stu said, swallowing his dose.

Shit, Jason thought. What did I just talk myself into?

Despite his initial hesitancy, once he got over the jolt of lift-off, Stu was fine. He kept rubbing his hands on his blue jeans, smiling, and saying, "Amazing."

After an indeterminate period of time, Stu suggested they step outside to view—that was his word, *view*—the stars with their *naked* eyes. Stars swirled like the hands on Jason's wristwatch. "The stars are amazing," Stu said. "It's amazing how much light they emit."

"Yes, right. *Amazing*," Jason replied, mimicking Stu. "The word for the day is *amazing*. Let's see how many times we can use it in a sentence before words fail us entirely."

Stu laughed good-naturedly. "I can't help it. Maybe I'm amazed."

Neither of them said much after that. They stood with their eyes glued to the heavens, each on his own trip, keeping each other company in silent comradery. After a time, Stu said, "I'm going inside for a while. Will you be OK out here by yourself?"

Amazing, Jason thought. While I was wondering how he was getting along with the acid, he was wondering about me. You never know what's going on in that guy's head. "I'm fine," Jason replied. "This is utterly amazing. The stars taste like sunshine."

"Then the sun will probably taste like starshine, but right now I'm going in to taste the soup," Stu said as he headed back to the cabin. Jason remained anchored to the ground. Soon a vaporous light began to flicker on the horizon. That must be the sunrise, Jason thought. He walked up a small hill where he had a view of the buildings that housed the two telescopes. He translated their fluted, domed roofs and cylindrical walls into lunar storage modules. The sky threw off creamy pinks and velvety indigos swirling together amidst a grey-blue background still saturated with stars. Blinding yellows and tangerines cascaded across the snow. The only footprints in sight were his.

Snow is crystalized rain, Jason thought, as he watched a gentle wind erase his footprints. Rain in another guise, an impermanent powdery apparition, nourishing the earth as it returns to its watery form.

He stood amidst absolute quiet. *Amazing*, he thought. The mountain itself moves, while the moon shifts in harmony and the stars remain stationary, and precipitation— in whatever form it takes—is the lubricant that eases the Earth's transition from night to day and back to night again, while I am but an observer, bearing scant witness, wandering the planet for a time, leaving as much evidence of the journey as my footprints do in the snow.

Jason was out there. He may as well have been on another planet. For all he knew, maybe he was. He was on some planet somewhere. But this was not the acid. No— this was his own insight, a sacred vision from deep within his consciousness, far from Emerald, far from the Jason who called himself Jason, far from the world he had known only hours ago.

Perhaps the purpose of life, he thought, the words coming together like interlocking puzzle pieces, is to see that there is no purpose . . . and that I must follow my own path even though there is no Path. There's no way I can tell anyone this. They'll think I'm nuts. But I'm going to remember.

The next morning Jason and Stu drove back to Emerald through the high desert covered in snow. Jason was now taking the blanketed mountains and prairies in stride, although everything straight was a little curly, and everything round was a little oval. He thought back to the conversation Stu had had with his two colleagues. Those

Accidental Destination

guys are *smart*, Jason thought. They crunch numbers like my feet crunch snow. Sky Noise. What a great name for a band. Or maybe Electric Sky Noise. Or just Electric Sky. I bet neither of them has ever done acid and never will. They don't need to. They're another breed entirely. Maybe it's time for me to stop doing it too. I've probably gotten everything out of it that I can.

"So, Stu—how was the soup?"

"It tasted like it came from a can, but I didn't need acid to tell me that."

"All right, then. How was your trip?"

"Interesting."

"Just interesting?"

Stu glanced at Jason. "Do you want me to say it?"

Jason caught Stu's eye. "A-maz-ing," they said in unison.

"Yeah. They always are," Jason replied.

The sage and bunchgrass of the flatlands gave way to pines and fir, and, in what seemed like minutes, Stu was dropping Jason off in Emerald.

Jason headed directly for Sophie's apartment, rather than his. While they weren't *officially* living together, the boundaries had blurred because they both had apartments in the same house. Jason had always wanted to live with a girl, but little by little, this sort of just happened, without any talk or fuss. The first words that tumbled out of his mouth as he walked through her door and wrapped his arms around her were "Soph, I've got it. I'm going to go to the university. That's the answer."

"I knew you'd figure it out. You'll do great. What's your major? I mean, what are you going to study?"

"I don't know."

"How about English? It makes sense. That's what you're interested in. You can get a PELL grant to cover your tuition and a Work-Study job and a student loan to live on."

"I don't know what they can teach me if I study English. I mean, I've already read a lot of books. But, yeah, that wouldn't be so bad. Getting paid to read books and write a few papers. It'd be a good scam. I'll get the ball rolling tomorrow morning."

15

THE APPLICATION PROCESS

As Jason walked onto the main part of campus, he realized that the university was much bigger than he had
thought, and that he didn't know where to apply. But the
building marked Administration looked like a good bet. He
climbed the oversized stairs slowly, for he had to take extra-
long strides to get up them. He passed between two pillars
the size of redwood trunks and pulled open one of the heavy,
polished brass-and-glass doors. The corridor was wider than
a two-lane highway and paved with green marble. Rows of
doors lined each side and two white marble staircases
veered off to the left and right, meeting at the landing on
the second floor.

Jason stood in the middle of the hallway. Men in suits
walked past him, paying him no attention. He looked up
and noticed that the ceiling was domed two stories above
his head where he saw a walkway and rows of doors similar
to those on the first floor. The entryway reminded him of a
state capitol building, whose architecture is designed to
symbolically dwarf the individual.

This may be a cold, faceless institution, Jason thought,
but you'd think they'd at least try to make it seem a little
more welcoming. No wonder The Professor back in Jersey
dropped out of that Ivy League school. And this is just a
state school. No wonder he opted for his own brand of *higher*

education. Maybe I don't belong in these *hallowed* halls.

Jason knocked on the first door on his left, marked with a plastic plaque reading *Interim Associate Provost*. No answer. He pulled the door open and found a woman in a business suit seated at a desk. "Excuse me," Jason said. "Where do I apply to go here for college?" She looked up and in an emotionless tone said, "Oh. You want *Admissions*. It's about two blocks up this street on the left. You can't miss it."

The admissions office was located in a small brick building that on the outside looked stately, but on the inside resembled the University Job Service more than it did the administration building. A woman seated behind a desk near the doorway looked up at him with a stone face. Behind her were rows of grey metal desks with what looked like students dressed in blue jeans and T-shirts, seated or moving about, shuffling folders and papers.

"Yes?"

"I'd like to apply to the university," Jason said.

The woman handed him a thick envelope. "Fill these out and make sure you include your transcripts and application fee. You can mail or bring it back here. You should fill out the grant and loan applications at the same time if you want to apply for those." She spoke without inflection, as if she had the instructions memorized.

The paperwork looked pretty straightforward. Jason filled it out that afternoon and dropped it in the mail the next day. Now all he had to do was wait.

That night he snuggled with Sophie in her bed. The room smelled like the hats of Southern belles and the jackets of Detroit gangsters. "What are you going to do with all these costumes after you graduate?" he asked. "Do they go back to the university?"

"No, they're all mine. I put them together little by little over the last few years. It's crazy how things accumulate. I should probably start boxing them up."

"What about *you*? You'll be gone well before school starts for me next September."

"I guess I will," she said, "—if that job in LA comes through."

"What about us? What's going to happens to us?"

She released him and sat up. "Do you care, Jason? Do you really care? You'll forget all about me after I'm gone."

He looked up at her and took her hands in his. "If I do, it'll take a long time. It'll take a long, long time."

She freed her hands and put them on her hips and pouted. "I know you don't really love me. You love that other girl."

She looked so silly, so cute. Was she acting? "What other girl?" he asked.

"I don't know. I just know there's someone else in your heart. I know I'm not the one. Oh Jason, why do we have to talk about the future? Can't we just have this while we have this?"

He put his hands around her waist, clasped them behind her and tilted his head so that she was looking him straight in the eyes. "Don't go all Zen on me now, Sophie. It takes two to tango, you know."

"OK then—let's tango." She bent down and kissed him the way she did that first night in the Caribou parking lot. "And when we're done *tangoing*, you can take me out for some ice cream."

"That organic stuff from the Creamery that comes from cows in their own pasture?"

"Oh yes, Sweetie," she whispered. "You know what I like."

Jason waited about two months with no word from the university about his application. Sophie's graduation had come and gone and he still wasn't sure where this thing of theirs was going. She could be maddeningly coy sometimes, as if time alone would work everything out and discussion was just wasted energy. "Why must we label everything?" she would respond whenever he tried to get serious about their relationship.

There's something she's holding back. I know there is, Jason thought. Maybe the fact that she's still here is telling me all I need to know. Maybe that job in LA will fall through and she won't have to bug out of Emerald. Maybe she isn't ready to abandon her dream and go back home to Wisconsin. She has to be hiding something, but who isn't? Whatever it is we have together, I don't want it to end yet.

The next morning, Jason and Sophie were eating breakfast in her kitchen. He swallowed the last bite of the mushroom and Swiss omelet she had served him. He was practically living there now. There was little reason for him to sleep upstairs in his studio. There was little reason for him to do very much of anything there. He picked up his coffee cup. "When school starts in the fall," he said, "I'd like to get my own place—not in a funky boarding house like this—but something nicer, you know, close to the university, maybe a duplex. You could stay with me—we could live together—you know, *officially*, for a while, until something turns up for you. And after that, who knows?"

"Such an offa, how could I refuse?" she replied in a mock Brooklynese accent, shrugging her shoulders and raising her upturned palms. "You'd better check on that application, then—you're not in yet. They don't let everyone in. They're very selective."

"I'm not worried. I'm a resident now. I'll get in."

"Don't be so sure." She gathered the dishes and put them in the sink. "If I were you, I'd check on it right away." She repeated the hand gesture. "What's witchya anyways?"

Was that a *yes*? Well, it wasn't a *no*, Jason thought. Once again, she wriggled out of answering. At the very least it's a definite *maybe*. I'll have to live with that. If I push it, I might get a definite *no*.

The next day, Jason returned to the admissions office and asked about his application. The woman behind the counter rolled her chair to a filing cabinet and pulled out a manila folder. "Your application is incomplete," she said. "We don't have your transcripts."

"They should have sent them."

"Well, we don't have them. Check with your high school and find out what happened. Tell them you need them to send us your transcripts."

"If they do, will I be able to get in for this fall?"

"Maybe. Get your transcripts in and we'll review your application. I can't do anything for you without them."

Jason called his old high school from a pay phone in the lobby and asked whether they had sent his transcripts.

"I'm sorry," the woman who had identified herself as the school secretary said, "but we don't give out that kind of information over the phone."

"But the college didn't get them. I need them right away. I went to school there. I need them to get into college. Can you at least tell me if you got a request for them?"

After a few more questions, Jason realized the woman wasn't going to help him, so he hung up. The university hadn't gotten his transcripts. He couldn't get any information about them either. That secretary had acted like it was top secret. At this point, Jason wasn't sure his high school even had any records on him, or, if they did, that his grades were good enough to get into the university. He had no idea what his grades were. He hadn't attended his graduation ceremony. Maybe I didn't even graduate at all, he thought. I probably cut more days than I spent in those cramped classrooms.

Jason returned empty-handed to the university admissions office. He knew they, too, had their protocols and no amount of negotiation was going to get him in without his transcripts. He explained the situation.

"What should I do now"? Jason asked.

"You could send another request and see what happens—or you could try the community college."

"What"?

"After a couple of semesters there, if you get good grades, you can reapply here."

"And I won't need my high school grades?"

"No. We'll just look at the community college transcripts. It looks like your PELL grant has been approved. You can ask them to pick it up. You're all set with that. And it looks like you're eligible for a federal student loan, no matter what school you attend. They'll facilitate that for you, too." She lowered her voice. "I probably shouldn't be telling you this—but it'll be a breeze. Believe me."

After all the waiting and runaround, this sounded good to Jason. To him, a school was a school and a PELL grant was a PELL grant. He had never been to the community college before, but he knew it was far enough out of town that he needed to drive or take the bus to get there. He hopped into his Galaxie and drove up the steep hill toward the college. The landscape was unremarkable until he crested a peak and saw the campus, isolate in the distance, framed by white clouds floating in front of a clear blue sky. *This* is the place for me, Jason thought.

He followed the signs to the college and pulled into the parking lot. There were plenty of spaces available. He didn't see any parking meters or signs warning that his car would be towed if he didn't have the proper sticker. There was one main building, and maybe two or three others behind it. No need to ask directions. He walked through the main doors into a large room and the admissions counter was right there, clearly marked. The enrollment services and financial aid areas were also clearly marked with large signs. Cardboard posters written in felt-tipped markers pointed the way to daycare and veterans services. Students—or soon-to-be students, Jason figured—were seated at tables, filling out forms and flipping through course catalogs.

Jason filled out the two-page application, wrote in the name of his high school and wrote *yes* in the box marked *Graduated*? He handed the form to a clerk, who briefly looked it over. She handed Jason a registration form and a course catalog. "OK. You're all set."

"That's it?" Jason asked. They just took my word that I graduated? Too easy, he thought.

"You can register right now," she replied. "If you like, you can speak to one of our advisors first. They're just down the hall."

"OK, thanks." I don't need an advisor, Jason thought. I can figure this out on my own. I'm just gonna take courses I'm interested in. He flipped through the catalog, which was filled with trades: accounting, culinary arts, electronics, welding, watershed science, forest biology . . . That's some serious stuff, Jason thought. Forest biology? That sounds

Accidental Destination

interesting, but I'm a musician, not a scientist. I wish I knew enough math to even consider that. Twelve bars of 1, 4, 5 equals the blues. That's all the math I know.

Hmmm . . . Introduction to Folklore looks interesting. But folklore ain't gonna get me no job. Jason heard himself slipping back into the street dialect of his youth, a dialect that had never been spoken in his home, but now, as it popped uninvited into his head, he was aware of how it would sound if it slipped out to, say, an admissions counselor or even Sophie, who liked to mimic his accent to an extreme. She never seemed to tire of asking him, "Ya wan dat cuppa caw-fee now?" And always with the hand gestures. Jason wiggled his toes. Maybe he did love that little pixie of a girl.

Automotive technology . . . Yeah. That old Galaxie of mine has about had it. Jason remembered that Marshall had been a mechanic in Ohio before he moved to Emerald and what he had said about why he had packed it in. "All the old men told me to get out while I was young, before rolling around on that damp concrete year after year turned me into an arthritic old cripple—and that's what I did."

Well, I don't have to kill myself sliding under cars, Jason thought. It'd be great to just have the knowledge—to know how cars work. It would be great to be able to fix cars, even if I don't get a job doing it. It'd be enough to know that I could if I had to. And if I live outside of town, it'd be essential. I know I fucked up trying to run that fucking press. But that experience has got to be worth something. Maybe I've got a bit more *aptitude* now. OK, then. Automotive technology it is.

Jason practically burst through Sophie's front door, wrapped his arms around her in a bear hug and lifted her off the floor. "Sophie—Sophie—I got into the community college! It's all set. I start next semester. I'm gonna move out of this boarding house and I'd like you to come with me. We could get us a waterbed—you know, a bed that's just ours—that no one else has slept on—and maybe one of those wicker papasan chairs that we both could scrunch up in."

He swung her around and put her down, still holding her close. "We talked about this before but now is the time— Let's do it! Don't go back to Wisconsin—please."

Sophie wriggled out from under his arms and clasped him in her own hug and pressed her lips to his. She kissed him quickly. One kiss after another. "Oh Jason," she said. "Now *that's* the way to ask a girl."

She had never looked more beautiful to him.

She grabbed his head and pulled it back the way she did whenever she was about to say something serious. She released him, sat on the edge of the bed and patted the space next to her. Jason sat down. She took his hands in hers.

"I can't fight this anymore," she said. "If we're gonna do this, we gotta do it smart." There she was with the accent again. She looked deep into his eyes and her voice got soft. "But I have to tell you something. I kinda have a boyfriend back in Baraboo. We've been together a long time."

"So you have a boyfriend." Jason was sick of girls telling him they *have a boyfriend*—as if to imply that that was the only reason they were rejecting him. "Well, someone better came along. It's not like you're married."

"But *he* thinks we're gonna get married someday. He's more like my best friend than a boyfriend and if I didn't meet you—I'd probably be . . .

"Anyway, you need to know this. He might call someday or even fly out here and try to—who knows what he'll do? But I'll take care of it. So I don't want you freaking out if he does. All right? He doesn't know about us. I'll try to let him down gently, but he might not give up so easily."

"All right," was all Jason could manage to say.

Sophie let go of Jason's hands and stood up. "And . . ." Her voice brightened. "Last week I was offered a job with The Little Theatre right here in town. It's a pathetic excuse for a hopelessly amateurish and provincial community theater. I didn't mention it because it was so ridiculous—but no one else has offered me a job and I know they haven't filled it yet. It's both administrative and artistic—I'd be running the show—literally. Maybe I could turn it into a place that serves up something more than dinner farces—

something with more depth."

She grabbed Jason's hands and began hopping up and down and running her words together. "What I'm saying is *Yes*, Jason—*Yes!* Let's do it. Let's *do it all*. Let's get that waterbed. Let's set up house. Let's see where this all goes. I love you, Jason. I loved you from the moment I saw you. You silly boy. I was just afraid to say it out loud and make it real. And if I hadn't come after you that night in the bar, who knows . . ." Her voice trailed off and she shrugged her shoulders.

"I think I love you too, Sophie. I really do." He noticed her hair was now a natural brown and her pixie cut had grown longer.

When the morning light spilled through the curtains, Jason and Sophie awoke simultaneously, still wrapped in each other's arms. "Wow," Jason said.

"Wow is right," she replied.

"There's still a month and a half left before school starts. I'm gonna head over to the Anthill and see if Vodka can set me up with a treeplanting gig so I can make a few bucks before school starts," Jason said.

"OK—and just one more thing. If I get pregnant, I'm having our baby. I want you to be clear about that. I've already had one abortion—I'm not going to have another."

"You won't get pregnant."

"That's what my sister said. She's already had three. I don't want to be like her. If you've ever had one, you'd know."

"Don't worry. We'll be careful. We don't need any rug rats running around."

Sophie pulled Jason close so that he could not see her face.

16

LIFE IS A CRUMMY RIDE

"You can't plant trees in July," Vodka said. "It's too dry. It hasn't rained all month and we probably won't get much until October. If you plant trees now, they'll just die. But our crew has a couple of spots open if you want to help us hand release some trees in up Sweet Creek next week." Vodka pressed his lips together and crinkled his eyes in the closest Jason had seen him come to a smile. "It's not as much fun as it sounds—it means scalping the ground in a three-foot square around some young trees. And cutting everything within six feet over it. You can start this Monday if you want. You just get yourself to the crummy and the crummy'll get us all to the site. Most of us just camp out there, but if you want to spend the time and energy going back and forth on your own every day, that's up to you. I don't advise it though."

"Just like that? You can hire me just like that?"

"Sure. Everyone deserves a chance. People drop like pine cones. I personally give you three days before you wash out. But that's because I know you. Others might not be so generous, but I know you and I know you're tougher than you look—for a city boy."

I'll show you—you pudgy little fuck, Jason thought, as he crunched his toes together hard.

Vodka began peeling the label off a bottle of Becks dark

Jason had brought and continued. "You'll technically be a guest worker, not an actual member of any crew. We're a cooperative, a worker-owned collective. Rusty calls this dump I'm crashing in a cooperative, but it's really not. He's a puppet master, the little man behind the curtain. He's probably socking away big bucks doing it—but anyway—this looks to be about a two-week job. Two weeks in the woods can be a long time, especially if you're not used to it. That's all this is—a job in the woods. It's not about *re*-forestation or *saving the planet one tree at a time* or whatever else you might think this is."

Vodka spoke as if saving the planet from becoming a blanket of concrete was the most distasteful thing imaginable. "You can't *re*-plant unless you've already ravaged the forest. What this is is hard work for good money—hopefully good money—outdoors in the woods—but in reality, we're in cahoots with the big corporations, enabling them to rape our forests while they dole out enough money for us to keep on living in shitholes like this season to season. That's what it is."

"You're quite the philosopher," Jason said.

Vodka eyed Jason's empty bottle as he took the final swig of his own beer. "Everyone has to believe in something. I believe I'll have another beer. You want one too?"

"No, thanks," Jason replied. "I've had three already. I've had enough. You've only had one."

Even with the nickname Vodka and the tales of his legendary benders, Jason had never seen him drunk or even take a sip of the clear elixir that had become his sobriquet. His buddies called him "Vod," but Jason didn't feel he had earned that right yet.

"That's the difference between you and me," Vodka said as he pried the top off another beer. "You drink fast and then call it quits. I drink slowly, but that allows me to keep drinking for a long time." He stared at Jason with those unblinking eyes and then looked off into the distance as if he were a great philosopher charged with imparting a cosmic truth to some youthful novitiate. Jason guessed this parable was one in which he was the hare and Vodka was the tortoise and that tortoise was looking into the near future, seeing himself savoring the remaining beers in the twelve-pack.

It's a small enough bribe to get the gig, Jason thought.

Jason drove his Galaxie—now sputtering and sucking up more gas than ever—to the pickup site. Following Vodka's instructions, he brought his sleeping bag and a daypack stuffed with the provisions he thought he'd need—peanut butter sandwiches, canned ravioli, tuna, water—all things that needed no refrigeration. When he saw the crummy, he knew where the vehicle had gotten its name. The old mini-bus, with wooden benches bolted to the floor where seats had once been, didn't look like it could start, much less carry a crew of ten with all their paraphernalia very far. It was an amalgam of bumps and scratches and dings held together with rust and duct tape. The hood was secured with a section of rope. I hope one of these guys knows something about keeping cars running, Jason thought. I don't want to cram into this *crummy* with all these characters and be stuck out somewhere between Emerald and East Jibib.

But climb aboard he did. If nothing else, this will be one hell of an experience, he told himself as he found an empty space on the bench running along the side of the vehicle, stashed his stuff between his legs and clutched it with his combat boots. What's the worst that could happen? he asked himself.

It took several tries and some skillful pumping of the gas pedal, as well as an extemporaneous invocation of the deities, to get the engine to turn over, but soon the crummy was chugging along the two-lane road out of town. The men were all bearded with long hair and the two women wore no make-up and were distinguishable from the men primarily by the fact that they had no beards. Their arms were every bit as muscled as the men's. In fact, to Jason's eye, they looked *exactly* like men's arms.

Jason noticed that someone had scratched LIFE IS A CRUMMY RIDE into the wooden bench. Well, this *is* a crummy ride, Jason thought. Literally. If this is a crummy, this must be a crummy ride. As the road turned to gravel and the tires spit out a cloud of soil and rock dust that looked like smoke, Jason continued his train of thought: I hope life *isn't* a crummy ride. Well . . . if life is an uncomfortable journey from one destination to another, life *could be* a crummy ride. I wonder if that's what the guy who carved this was getting at.

As the crummy pulled into the job site, Jason saw an array of tents, campers, pick-ups with shells, plastic lean-to's and even a tipi. Before he could reach any conclusion about this, he stepped out of the crummy and craned his neck to gaze up at the mountain. It looked like a battlefield covered with trees planted in rows, spaced at about six feet in all directions. Logs and sawed-off branches were cocked at various angles, rock outcroppings broke up the lines of trees, and the trees themselves were smothering in brush. And it was steep. Very steep.

"It looks a little bushy," Vodka said, suddenly appearing beside Jason. "The BLM thinks these saplings need a little help to survive and I can't say I disagree." Jason knew from the many conversations at the Anthill that BLM stood for the Bureau of Land Management or—as Vodka liked to call it—the Bureau of Land Manglement. He handed Jason a hoedad, a pair of loppers for cutting overhead brush, and a hard hat. "A lot of guys don't wear these, but *you'd* better. And if you see a log or boulder rolling down the mountain at you—don't just turn and run. Take a second to watch where it's going and *then* move to avoid it. And for now, don't look up. It's all about the tree you're working on right now. Take this line next to mine," he said, pointing at a column of trees, "and try to keep up. And when you get to the top, don't look down." Nearly everyone had said that Vodka was a falling down drunk and was about to get kicked off the crew—if he lived that long—but at this moment he looked to Jason like a Bodhisattva in flannel and caulk boots.

Jason had been told that he had about three minutes to scalp each tree and cut the overhead brush. Thirty minutes had elapsed. He had only done six. His calves and shoulders were already beginning to ache. He glanced over at Vodka and it looked like he was keeping pace with him, but he knew Vodka had to be hanging back. "It doesn't have to be beautiful," Vodka yelled over. "Just fulfill the requirements so it passes inspection—and fer Chrissake don't stand there admiring your work." Then he was gone, catching up to the rest of the crew.

Jason looked up and saw the crew was way ahead of him. They worked fast and efficiently, working together without seeming to work together—and with no boss. There was a cohesion that Jason hadn't seen with the incongruous assortment of characters that had made up his CETA "crew."

He wished he had brought along a better pair of gloves. First chance I get I'll pick up some leather ones. These canvas ones were false economy, he thought, as he felt the blisters beneath the already torn cloth.

How long have I been pounding this dry ground? Jason wondered as the steel of his hoedad ricocheted off another rock. He was thirsty and hungry, muscles he didn't even know he had ached, and he'd probably be cut loose for being so slow. By sheer strength of will, he made it through the day. He had heard horror stories of waterlogged treeplanters who never dry out from the winter rains and grow webbing between their toes, but this had to be as bad. He was dusty through his clothes, scratched and pricked from God knows what and his hands were either numb or on fire, he didn't know which. He wasn't about to try to catch a ride back to town and then come all the way back here again tomorrow.

It's a nice enough night, he thought. I'll just unroll my sleeping bag somewhere out of the way and crash. He removed his boots and socks and crawled into his bag, but when he closed his eyes, his slumber was uneasy. He saw the mountain with its trees full grown reaching for the stars and moon, creating a haven for wildlife and nature spirits. Decades passed like minutes. He felt the wind and rain and snow and sun simultaneously nourish what had moments before been this clearcut with its struggling, choked saplings.

Jason felt a boot gently resting on his left leg and heard a woman's voice: "Hey Greenhorn—time to chow down. Get over there and help yourself to some scrambled eggs and oatmeal before it's all gone." By the time he opened his eyes, she was gone, and he wondered if she too had been part of his dream.

It was barely beginning to get light when Jason walked over to the fire, toward the smell of coffee. Someone handed him a bowl filled with eggs and oatmeal. "Hey . . . thanks," Jason said.

"We're a team," someone replied.

"Yeah," said another. "All kinds of shit hits the latrine out here in the woods. We gotta work together to get the job done. It's just us against the elements and—more often than not—the FS inspectors." He must have seen Jason crinkle his eye. "That's *forest service*, man," he added.

Two days, three days, Friday, one week. Jason was packing up to head back to Emerald to find a laundromat, pick up some more socks, a water bottle he could clip to his belt and a hundred other things he hadn't known he needed, including his own cup for morning coffee. His boots had held up though. They weren't those cleated caulks that cost those hardcore high rollers a week's worth of wages. They were just a pair of government-issue jungle boots that had cost him next to nothing at a military surplus store in New Jersey. Uncle Sam knows what he's doing, Jason thought, as he climbed into the crummy, barely able to lift his legs to step up into the vehicle. I don't know how I made it through a whole week. These guys are something else. They're serious and in great shape. I must have lost ten pounds that I didn't have to lose in the first place. But I feel so alive. I can't explain it. I didn't expect this feeling. It's got to be more than the adrenaline. This has got to be as good as any CIA acid. Maybe the repetition of the climbing and the motion of the hoedad is the key to this koan. Maybe the answer is there is no answer.

"I'm tired, but I feel OK," was all Jason could verbalize of his feelings when someone asked how he was doing.

"What doesn't kill us makes us stronger," said the

planter with the German accent who was crammed in next to him. The crummy was choked with litter and smelly clothes and Jason didn't want to begin to think what else, but it probably included several varieties of malevolent microbial organisms and more than a few critters large enough to be visible to the naked eye if they crawled out from their hiding places. But Jason didn't care. He was headed back to Emerald and Sophie. He was going to shower, take her out to a big dinner and fuck the stuffing out of her—preferably not in that order.

"Where's Vodka? Jason asked.

"Dunno."

"Haven't seen him."

"No one really cares," said another.

"We packed him back to town yesterday morning," said Rainbow, the woman who had cooked for the crew and offered Jason breakfast earlier in the week. She also worked on the slopes during the day and left most of the men in the dust.

"Why?" Jason asked.

"Every night he pulls out a pint of vodka and drinks till he passes out somewhere around the perimeter," she said. "If a pint doesn't do it, he pulls out another. Usually after two days on the job, he can't be here anymore. It's too dangerous. We don't want him falling into a ditch or off the mountain, so we send him home. He protests a bit, but he goes. Then he nurses beers at that ant hole he crawls into until he sobers up enough to hang on to a hoedad again. He'll be back next week and the same thing will happen. It'll be *déjà vu* all over again."

"Then why do you let him come out with you?"

She shrugged as the crummy lurched forward around a sharp curve.

I guess all those stories *are* true, Jason thought. He had never seen Vodka out of control, or even out of the Anthill until this week, but he had not only gotten Jason on the crew, he had also stuck with him long enough to make sure he got through the first day. Not exactly an act of redemption, but an act of kindness that should count for something.

"He stored up a lot of good karma when he saved a guy's life on a fire crew in Colorado a couple of summers back," said a man with a bushy beard, lighting a cigarette with a book of matches embossed with a silver marijuana leaf and the slogan "Freedom is the Issue." He threw the match on the floor and exhaled. "Pushed him out of the way of a burning log. Almost crispy-crittered himself while watching two others burn up. He won't talk about it though. The only reason I know is I was on the crew that mopped up after him."

"Yeah, but Vod's still a fuck-up," said another man as he adjusted his suspenders before spitting tobacco into an empty beer bottle.

"Let's face it—we're all fuck-ups one way or another—or we wouldn't be here. We'd be that college *edu-macated* inspector perched on the slopes holding a clipboard instead of a hoedad who thinks a clear-cut is still a forest. I'd think that too if I was brainwashed by all that book *larnin'* and getting paid what he is."

Rainbow caught Jason's eye, held it for a moment, and then shrugged again.

Jason spent most of the next two days in bed. His fingers were blistered. Not guitar-playing blistered, but *seriously* blistered. His hands were swollen, but the blisters, scrapes and cuts on his feet and legs took his mind off them. He began to put together the changes of clothes that he would need to get him through the next week. "You don't have to go back," Sophie said when he moaned involuntarily as he lifted a gallon jug of water.

"Yes, I do."

"Why? You've fulfilled your tree-planting fantasy."

Jason ignored the part about what he was doing being tree *planting*. "No. The crew needs me. We have to knock out that unit by next Friday or we could default on the contract."

"*Knock out that unit? Default on the contract?* Do you hear yourself? You don't owe them anything. Do what you want, but don't forget you have that blues jam next Friday night. And that bitch Laredo will fire you if you don't show.

And I wouldn't blame her. You *never* miss a gig."

"I know. I can't explain it, but I've got to do this. I'm not a quitter." Jason thought of the mountain he had trudged up and down. Without even closing his eyes, he saw the lines of trees that wouldn't have had a chance to reach maturity without his hoedad work. He smelled the pines and the cramped, ratty, Vodka-less crummy and knew that most especially he had to do it for Vodka.

Vod might be a fuck-up, Jason thought, but I'll be damned if I'm going to be the one to let him bring a washout to the crew.

"No one's calling you a quitter," Sophie said.

"I know," Jason replied, "but we could use the money for our new place."

It didn't take long for Jason and Sophie to find an apartment on the Southside, near where Jason had spent many pleasant hours glued to McCann the Acid Man's couch smoking primo bud. The neighborhood was more upscale than the Westside where they were moving from. Here, they could walk to an organic food store and a coffee shop where they could sit outside and drink espresso and munch fancy fresh pastries. It was much nicer than anywhere Jason had ever lived, and he felt out of place.

"This is nice," Sophie said when she walked into the empty apartment. "There's lots of light and it's a lot closer to my theater and your school. It won't take long to fix this place up nicely—you'll see."

Jason paid the deposit and rent with cash. "You really need to get a checking account now, Sweetie," Sophie said. "Only poor people pay for things with cash."

Soon the apartment was filled with enough furniture to live comfortably. It was cheap stuff, mostly snagged from thrift stores for next to nothing, stuff that would as likely as not be left behind in any major move, but it looked good because of Sophie's embellishments with accents of fabric and wall coverings.

Jason bought that new waterbed and splurged on a set of purple silk sheets. "Have you ever made love on a waterbed before?" he asked, wrapping his arms around Sophie's waist and pulling her close.

"Sweetie, where I come from even the dogs have waterbeds," she replied.

One evening, shortly before his classes were set to begin, Jason sat in his papasan chair, looked around at the apartment and thought of all those little touches that only a woman can bring to a home—that Sophie had brought to *their* home. The clear glass canisters of macaronis on the kitchen counter, the fact that the bed was made, the boxes of make-up and jewelry on the dresser . . . He had never had a girlfriend that he lived with day in and day out—one he ate, slept, fucked and made love with—and he liked it. He liked it a lot. He had it all—he had a girlfriend, an apartment, a car, some money coming in . . .

Now, all I have to do is not fuck this all up, he told himself.

17

SHIFTING GEARS

Jason sat in the classroom listening to the instructor introduce the course on engines while some of his classmates tried to cajole him into talking about how to modify them for racing—something that apparently this guy was known for. The brightness of the fluorescent lights directly above the rows of tables pushed together gave the basement classroom a distinctly corporate feel, more like attending a training session at his old insurance company than sitting in a college class. Many of his classmates looked like they had stepped out of garages and tire repair shops—in fact, several of them were wearing work shirts with iron-on nametags. The student on his right, a Chicano named Carlos, dressed in black denim and wore a blue cotton bandana wrapped around his forehead. The student on his left wore a polyester Hawaiian-style shirt, a perfectly coiffed shag haircut and a neatly trimmed beard. I wonder what *he's* doing here, Jason thought. He noticed that most of the students didn't have textbooks. He idly flipped through his, wondering how students could get through a class without them.

Jason found it hard to concentrate on the soft-spoken instructor who was droning on, reading the syllabus word for word. His mind wandered back to the Caribou Bar on the last scheduled blues night. He had walked in aching, dead tired from the forest, barely able to lift his bass and amp—a brand new one that he had not even used at a gig yet, and found Mitchell—with his drum kit still unpacked—seated at a table, looking like he had been there all afternoon. "I don't know, man," Mitch mumbled, staring down at his beer. "She's in the wind. It was good while it lasted though, wu'en't it?"

"What happened?" Jason asked.

"Who knows? Some cock-and-bull story about her cover being blown. With her you never know. It could be anything."

"But—hey, *we're* here. Maybe could just play casually behind whoever shows up. I mean, we're still the rhythm section, right? It might be fun."

"Yeah," Mitch replied. "But she's got the PA."

Jason sighed loudly. "It was good while it lasted though, wu'en't it?" he said, mimicking Mitch's accent.

Mitch stood up and saluted Jason with his bottle of beer. "That bartender du'en't look none too happy about it neither. We'd better skee-daddle. Good knowin' ya, man. She'll slink back to town one of these days—but we'll never play here again."

The air conditioner stopped abruptly, and Jason opened his eyes and looked around the windowless classroom. His fingers caressed his daypack's zipper and he wondered what type of lunch Sophie had packed for him. They'd sure come a long way since that first night in the Caribou Bar.

The instructor, Mr. Hewitt, was now warning the class about the dangers of carbon monoxide. "I used to walk into my shop when all the engines were running, take a deep breath and say, 'Mmmm, this smells *goooood*.'" He demonstrated by inhaling deeply, holding his breath and pounding on his chest with his fist. "I've breathed in so much of it over the years, that now it makes me sick to breath in even a little. Don't let the same thing happen to you. When we're in the shop, make sure the exhaust hoses are always hooked up whenever you run an engine."

"Shit. Fuck. Piss, mon," Carlos said. "Just get on with it." Apparently Mr. Hewitt's hearing isn't that good either,

Jason thought, because he continued without missing a beat.

The student in the Hawaiian shirt raised his hand and, without waiting to be called on, asked, "When you were on Garner's crew at Daytona, what was his cam's lift ratio?"

"Don't try to draw me into that, Eddie," Mr. Hewitt replied, with the trace of a smile. "We have to stick to the basics here. We've got a lot of ground to cover and not a lot of time to do it in. When you rebuild your own engines, you might be able to modify them *slightly*."

Holy shit, Jason thought. I have to *rebuild* an engine?

That afternoon, the class met in the lab—twenty workstations in a circle—some with engines already on hoists, others with the hoists empty. The engine area was surrounded by a wire-mesh cage. This was located in an even larger room with separate areas for working on transmissions, brakes and the like. All in all, the basement workshop looked very *industrial* to Jason, with its concrete floor, bay doors and equipment storage lockers. I might as well be working in a garage right now, he thought.

Jason noticed that the engines were different sizes and he marveled at that. This had to be the case, he knew, but to actually see them next to each other startled him. A couple of students were gawking at a particularly large engine. "I love these big-block V-8s," one said, resting his hand lightly on top of it. "Take a look at the size of that intake manifold," the other replied. It sounded to Jason like they were ogling a pretty girl.

Jason stared at the engine. He had learned earlier that day that engines had something called *manifolds* and that they came in both the intake and exhaust varieties. He was proud of this newfound knowledge and thought he'd show it off, although he would have been hard pressed to point out either type. "I can't tell an *intake* manifold from an *exhaust* manifold," he said.

"Well then, you shouldn't be in this class," another student replied.

"I'm studying this because I *don't* know it," Jason said. "If *you're* so smart, maybe *you* shouldn't be here."

The manifold expert cocked his head to the side, and appeared to be sizing Jason up, planning his next move.

Eddie smirked. "Don't worry about these *gearheads*," he said, turning and resting his hand gently on Jason's back, guiding him away. "If you want, you can partner up with me. I'm rebuilding a Dodge Super Bee from the shell up and I'm just here so I have somewhere to work on my engine. Stick with me and I'll get you through this lab."

"Yeah, man. Cool," Jason replied. "But why?"

"We freaks gotta stick together. These rednecks all they wanna do is twist nuts in a Ford dealership somewhere. I'm here so I can drive exactly the car I want. I've got a need for speed. I can't drive 55."

"You all have the choice to rebuild either your own engine or one we supply," Mr. Hewitt said. "If you choose to rebuild your own, you *will* have to fire it up at the end of the semester in order to pass this course."

Shit, Jason thought. Not only do I have to rebuild an engine, it has to work too?

"And parts will be expensive. Even if you plan on it being more expensive than you think it will be, it will be more expensive than that, even factoring in that you planned on it being more expensive than you thought it'd be. You're always going to need another something or other."

Jason stuck it out, tentatively tightening bolts with a torque wrench, gapping spark plugs, removing old piston rings and whatever else Eddie directed him to try. Jason sometimes hung out with him after class, smoking pot from a dragon-shaped ceramic bong and watching him tinker with his Super Bee, which he kept propped up on jack stands, no headlights, no rear tires, and going nowhere fast from the looks of things.

Eddie also did cheapo cheapo word-of-mouth tune ups for the price of parts and what a Quick Change shop charged for an oil change alone. Watching Eddie work was like watching a one-man pit crew in the middle of a race. He changed the oil, gapped the plugs and set the points, checked the distributor cap for pitting and the air filter for dirt in less time than it took a regular shop to just change the oil. Jason couldn't believe that he got away with all this in the parking lot below his apartment building, but what amazed him the most was that Eddie never spilled a drop of oil on the concrete floor.

"This is who I am," Eddie said. "I'm nothing more than a pot-smoking, polyester-loving grease monkey. My dad used to restore old cars and he had me draining oil pans before I could ride a tricycle." He replaced the oil cap, reached in through the driver side window and turned the key on the Honda he had just finished working on. "This rice burner sounds like an oversized lawnmower, but I've got it sounding as sweet as it ever will."

At the end of the semester, Eddie and Jason stood admiring their completed engine. "It looks great, right down to the custom painted, sparkle valve covers," Jason said.

"Yeah, but the real beauty is inside where you can't see it—the three-quarter cam and bored-out cylinders," Eddie replied. He fired it up, and the bubbling roar sounded good even to Jason, who had no idea what a V8-440 was supposed to sound like, raw and unmuffled, but, in comparison, most of the other engines sounded like little firecrackers popping, straining to go off. A couple of the engines wouldn't start at all.

When he heard Eddie's engine, Mr. Hewitt, as low-key as ever, made a check mark on his clipboard and said, "Well done, but it sounds like it might be a *little* out of spec."

One student nudged another and said, "Yeah—*a little*. Yours sounded like a wet frog fart next to Eddie's."

"Did you hear that?" another said as the engine continued to swing on the hoist's chains. "That eight-banger's headed straight for the finish line."

"She's bored and stroked all right. I can't wait to drop her into Aunt Bee," Eddie said to no one in particular.

"You're the muscle *and* the brains of this outfit," Jason said to Eddie. "You got the gift, man. Thanks for getting me through the semester."

"No problem, bro," Eddie replied, looking to Jason like a

rock star—tall and lean with mutton-chop sideburns, tinted shades, snakeskin boots and a shiny gold shirt, half unbuttoned. Jason knew he had dressed this way for the occasion. Why can't I meet musicians like Eddie? Jason wondered.

"Are you two *maricóns* gonna hug each other now or would you rather hump the engine?" Carlos asked. He always had a joke to share and seemed unconcerned about grades or lab work. "Hey Eddieman—tomorrow night some of us are having a par-tay to celebrate the end of *ese* semestray. We're gonna have a keg and a bonfire and—*quién sabe*—who knows what all else. A real Mex-i-can blowout like you've never seen."

"Far out," Eddie replied. "And I can bring a little something *extra*, something *special*, if you know what I mean. We're gonna get reallly fuuuuuckt uuuuuup."

"*¡¡Siiiii…moannnnn!!*" Carlos replied, snapping his index and middle fingers together and shaking his head vigorously up and down, before giving Scott the double thumbs up.

Mr. Hewitt appeared out of nowhere, stood in front of them and spoke quietly: "I don't know why you boys want to blow your minds. You have so little to begin with." He then looked at the floor and shook his head slowly from side to side as he walked away.

Shit, Jason thought. What am I doing here? This is an even bigger disaster than the print shop. I know I could have run a press if I had had just a little more time or luck or *something*—but *cars*? What the hell was I thinking?

"Hey *ese*," Carlos said to Jason. "You should come too."

Seriously, what *am* I doing here? Jason asked himself again. I have nothing in common with any of these guys. Eddie's a rich stoner from Lake Oswego and he only wants me around to hand him his tools or help him harf a transmission or whatever into place on that wreck of his he's rebuilding. What a piece of crap. With its faded paint and dings, it looks more like a pace car for a treeplanters' crummy parade than something anyone would want to be seen driving. And now he's going to hide that beautiful engine in it. I've been at this a whole semester and all I know for sure about cars is that you have to keep them full of fluids.

"Yeah. Maybe I will," Jason replied.

As Jason was registering for the next semester's courses, Introduction to Folklore caught his eye again. I *have* to take that, he thought. But it conflicts with my automotive schedule and I'd have to take the lab in the morning instead of the afternoon, which means Eddie won't be able to help me. I'll fail the lab for sure. No way I can rebuild a transmission all by myself. *Fuck it.* The teacher plays fiddle with that all-girl Irish group, We Lasses. I gotta take her class. I'll sign up for that and whatever other courses look interesting. I still get my grant no matter what I take as long as I have at least twelve credits. Fuck auto tech.

So he signed up for the folklore class as well as Introduction to Psychology, French I, and a couple of others.

"*Now* you're being smart," Sophie said when he told her he was dropping out of the automotive cluster. "The academic classes will count for something when you transfer to the university and you'll have a much more enjoyable college experience now. I don't know what your obsession is with the blue-collar lifestyle. Besides, you've got such big, beautiful hands. You don't want to go scarring them up for nothing."

"I never thought of it like that. I was just trying to learn some sort of trade, so I could maybe, you know . . . but right now, I'm just gonna collect my financial aid and study things I like and concentrate on my writing and music."

"That's the way to do it. Look at me—I combined my art with an employable skill, such as it is."

"*You're* the smart one," Jason said, as he wrapped his hands around her waist and kissed her neck.

"Let go of me," Sophie said, smiling and gently pushing him away. "I have to finish cooking dinner."

As he waited for dinner to be served, Jason slouched down in his papasan chair, cradled his Telecaster bass and thought of Jenny. He hadn't thought of her in a long time. Why am I thinking of her now? he asked himself. Maybe it's the bass. We had something once, but that was all fun and games—not real like this.

Jason closed his eyes and hugged his bass tight. He remembered his last days of lovemaking with Jenny after she said that she had to go away for a while—slow and passionate, as if each time could be the last. I get laid every day now—more than every day, really. It isn't the same as with Jenny, but things have changed, Jason thought, as he relaxed his toes and began to doze off.

18

LITERARY LIONESSES

After his first folklore class, Jason looked forward to going to school each day. It didn't hurt that his instructor looked like a star, with red curly hair to the middle of her back—a bona fide professional musician who demonstrated variations of Irish folk tunes on the fiddle and let him call her Colleen. But he would have looked forward to class even if Mr. Hewitt had been teaching it. Jason learned that tales of animal tricksters like Brer Rabbit were often thinly disguised narratives of blacks on the plantations getting over on the white man. He learned that the weather on the coast was the result of an agreement between the wren and the North Wind. He learned that technically none of the songs he sang were folk songs.

Classes were a breeze and although he didn't really work that hard, Jason consistently made A's on his tests and essays. He was usually confident he had an A before he turned them in. Not only did he do well on his essays, but he enjoyed writing them. He wrote one for psych class about dreams, whether they were a gateway into a higher consciousness or merely the random firing of synapses, and he revised it far beyond what he knew was necessary for A-level work. He was as meticulous with his essays as he was with his songwriting.

Classes met above ground in the main building and he

now mingled with a variety of students. Although he was a few years older than most of them, this was the college experience he had envisioned when he first set foot on the university campus with Susie. He learned how to ask for directions in French to both the library and the bookstore, and he imagined studying abroad in Paris for a semester. He filled his plate to overflowing at the salad bar and sometimes splurged on a flaky croissant in the cafeteria, although he knew he couldn't afford it. The fact that going to school in the first place had begun as a scam was quickly becoming secondary.

And he still had plenty of time to play music with Tim and Marshall, although he felt guilty jamming with them as much as he did, rather than seeking out musicians who wanted to play professionally. Wasn't he weary enough of their cover songs and his unraveling relationship with Tim?

They had never spoken of that night at the Boarding House, but every time Jason looked at Tim he saw that desperate urchin clinging to this cheater who had probably forgotten all about her by now. And he saw Marshall as an inarticulate, self-satisfied redneck with a huge talent he didn't appreciate going to waste. Jason had never gotten over him fucking Susie, although he knew he had no cause to be jealous. She could turn on the charm and make any man lose his brains. And hadn't she warned him that Marshall would be just another one among many? Plenty of time had elapsed since then. I guess you never forget your first zipless fuck, Jason thought.

But Jason loved music. No matter where you play it or with whom, it dissipates like vapor. And isn't all life like that? Transient. Impossible to grasp and foolhardy to try. So what difference does it make, he thought, where I play, who I play with, or even what I'm playing, as long as I am playing? It's the music—not the song or the musicians—that matters. But even so, he asked himself, are these two guys really the best I can do?

Between classes, Jason hung in the office where the school's literary magazine was produced. The room was furnished with a couple of desks, a coffee maker, a few chairs,

Accidental Destination

a bookcase with an assortment of literary magazines from around the country and a poster advertising the movie *One Flew Over the Cuckoo's Nest*. People came and went on no discernible schedule and someone was almost always there, scribbling in a notebook or going on about some book they were reading.

Clare, the pock-marked, chain-smoking poetry editor, was in Jason's French I class. They had gotten to talking about poetry—she said loved she Baudelaire, and he replied that he didn't think there was an English translation that did him justice. (He failed to mention that he didn't speak enough French to know this, and she failed to question how someone taking French I could reach this conclusion.)

He quickly became a fixture in the office after pointing out that no progress was being made on producing the camera-ready art they needed for the printer and that he would be happy to help them with it.

This year's staff was comprised of five people, all women, all editors, all with impressive titles. The managing editor was paid with Work-Study funds and all she had to do was produce a single journal in two semesters. This is my kind of scam, Jason thought.

The first order of business for this new crew had been to change the journal's name. They spent weeks kicking around various possibilities before agreeing on *Shasta*. "The name needed changing," the managing editor said. "It's been around for twenty years with the same old boring name—*The Emerald Review*."

"I like that *Shasta*'s a strong, single word with so many layers of meaning," Clare said.

I like that you don't know or care that the mountain's not even located in this state, Jason thought.

All of the poems Jason had submitted for publication had been rejected, and most of the selections for the upcoming issue had been contributed by the staff members themselves.

"Hey—" Clare had said when Jason pointed this out to her, "*We're* the one's who have the vision for the journal and *we're* the one's putting our names on it." Although it seemed to Jason that her two major contributions were channeling a driveling imitation of Ann Sexton's confessional style and rejecting his own poetry, she did have a point.

He admired their self-confidence. No matter what I or anyone else think of this little magazine, the editors' reputations are on the line, Jason thought. I don't think much of the poetry or the stories they're running, but it's their gig. I'm just enjoying the show. This beats working in a print shop by a mile.

The light table was buried under books and papers, Jason didn't see the correct size boards or any non-repro blue graph paper, and they certainly didn't have a wax machine—or even any glue sticks from the looks of things—to paste up the layout. I'm not even sure, Jason thought, that they know this *is* a light table. When they passed out their fancy titles, they didn't think to name someone to actually produce this rag. Did they expect some printer's devil to come in the middle of the night and the journals would magically appear the next morning?

"You know," Jason said, "we'd better get a move on getting this ready for the printer. The first thing we need to do is send all this text out to be typeset. We have a lot of decisions to make. Like margin sizes and what fonts and leading we want."

The editors may as well have been listening to an astrophysicist lecture on the variations in light output when measuring the spectra of stars. No one said a word. "We might want to track out the titles, but we don't have to decide that now. Have you thought about what style of hyphenation and justification you'd like?" Jason was now messing with them, but he couldn't help it. "Don't worry," he said. "I learned how to do all this stuff when I worked at Lasting Impression."

Jason had never actually produced any camera-ready boards, but he had seen enough of them to know he could do it. He had seen a lot of sloppy ones come through the door, so he knew what to look out for. The rule at the shop was that you don't change the customer's art. If you notice a typo or a pagination error, too bad—keep your mouth shut and run it as provided. Sloppy errors shouldn't be a problem here, he thought. These guys'll go over their own poems and stories so many times they'll wear the words off the pages with their eyeballs. If there's a typo, it'll be something big, like getting the volume and issue numbers wrong.

Once the typeset texts arrived, Jason could have pasted the boards up in a couple of days. But he hemmed and hawed and made the process seem a lot more complicated than it really was. He enjoyed pulling out the line gauge he had inherited from the print shop, making a show of measuring nothing in particular, and then appearing to reposition it slightly while the editors watched, confusing his slapstick performance with expertise.

One day, Jason was named associate poetry editor by consensus when he suggested that a particular poem could benefit from a stanza break. He didn't say that the reason for the break had more to do with page design than improving the poem itself, which he thought was a lost cause. It possibly started as a joke when Sylvia, the managing editor—or editor in chief—or whatever she was calling herself that day—chuckled and said, "Maybe we should promote you to associate poetry editor."

Jason didn't miss a beat. "Sure. Let's do it. How about it everybody?"

"Sure, why not?"

"Fine with me."

"OK," Sylvia said. "Then you'll have to put one of your own poems in, if you can find room. If you're going be an editor, you have to showcase your work. How about one of those poems with the words scattered all over the page? Maybe that one about the Rose Garden. Any one you can shoehorn in is fine with me. Just run it by Clare."

It's not who ya know, it's who ya blow, Jason thought, as he sliced the poem apart with a razor knife.

When the boards were finished, Jason hand delivered them to the printer, and anticipation built as everyone waited for the first proofs, a sample of what the finished product would look like.

Correcting them had been a Hungarian clusterfuck, with

each of the other five editors clamoring to make *just one more little change*—usually on their own stories or poems.

When the journals arrived from the print shop, Sylvia was the first to rip a box open. "They look great!" she exclaimed, as everybody dug in, scooping up handfuls of copies for themselves.

This is the power of the press I felt when I first walked into Lasting Impression, Jason thought. But if writers have the goods, they can staple together mimeographed sheets and hand them out at the Saturday Market for all the difference it makes. The power is not in the press, but in the words and ideas. The medium is *not* the message. The message is the message.

But this was no mimeo handout. This was professionally printed and bound. And it looked beautiful. "This looks better than Kesey's *Spit in the Ocean*," Jason said, holding up a copy of each side by side. But of course what *Spit* may lack in production values, it more than makes up for in quality of writing, he thought. Kesey was beyond measuring margins.

"We need to have a reading," Clare said.

"Yes—let's do it," said the fiction editor.

"We could probably get the art gallery downtown to let us use their space for free some night," Sylvia said.

"And I can be the master of ceremonies," Jason said. "My girlfriend runs The Little Theatre. I'm sure she can set me up with a tuxedo. It'll be a trip."

Jason appeared at the reading in a powder blue tux with wide shiny lapels and dark fuzzy stripes down the sides of the legs. To this, Sophie had added a paisley cummerbund and a salmon-colored ruffled shirt with French cuffs. "Your new white canvas sneakers will complete the outfit nicely," she had said. He thought they added just the right touch of incongruity to an already outrageous costume.

Jason surveyed the paintings, the track lighting and the hardwood floors of the art gallery and thought this could turn into a *happening*, like the first performance of "Howl" in San Francisco. Not on the same scale, of course—not with these poems—but it could be the start of something, a way to get the writers and poets of Emerald all together. He wished that Sophie could have been here, but she was busy with a rehearsal at the theater. "I'm sorry, Sweetie," she had said. "You know I'd love to make it, but I just can't. Without me, there'd be no rehearsal." Jason understood, but this didn't change the fact that she wasn't here.

Jason set up the microphone and amplifier. Sylvia arranged the cheese and crackers on a card table. They didn't skimp on the Burgundy. After all, red wine was what writers drank. Sylvia twisted the cap off a jug and began swigging directly from the bottle. Clare stacked copies of the journal near the snack table as gifts for the guests. She popped a cassette into her portable recorder to tape the event.

Guests began arriving, mostly friends of the readers, but also some who had heard of the event through flyers posted around the college and town. There must have been close to thirty people. No one had thought to bring chairs, so the audience milled about, standing in small groups.

When it was time for the reading, Jason stepped to the microphone, which was little more than a prop since the acoustics were good in the small gallery, and began: "Ladies and gentlemen, welcome to the *Shasta* literary journal's poetry and fiction reading, presented in cooperation with Emerald Community College . . ."

People sat in clusters on the floor. Jason hammed it up like he was on stage at the Caribou emceeing a music revue, except that here the crowd was quiet, attentive, and sipped wine from plastic cups rather than hollering and spilling mugs of beer on the floor.

Jason began the reading with a poem by a Vietnamese poet longing for the wind to bring a new season to a farmer resting under a banyan tree. "Is this the enemy?" Jason asked. The audience applauded enthusiastically as he introduced each reader, exaggerating their accomplishments and encouraging the crowd to give each of them a hearty round of applause, which, Jason knew, they would.

After several monotone readers whose only virtue was

that they were so nervous they blew through their poems rapidly, Clare surprised Jason with a performance that brought her native North Dakota to life. Its thunderstorms, red fox in the grasslands and glacial past, which lay lifeless and sentimental on the page, materialized in multiple dimensions. Spirits of the indigenous Ojibwe and Dakota Sioux, conjured by name, hung in the air and took form on her breath. Clare shouted, shook, whispered and tapped on a hand drum. This was not the Clare Jason knew. These were not the poems Clare had published. After Clare, the other poets sounded alike, nattering on about love in its various unfulfilled permutations—longed for, lost, fleeting and unrequited—as Jason became progressively more buzzed on wine and adrenaline and the reading drew to a close.

As the editors were saying goodbye to the guests and signing copies of the journals, Jason picked up a broom and Clare said, "When we get out of here, drop by my place. That's where the real party will be."

"Sounds good," Jason replied. "The after-party's often the best part of a show."

"No it's not," Clare said. "It's the applause we get after we read."

"Yeah. I didn't think of that. Maybe we should have called all the readers up at the end for a kind of curtain call. But that would have emptied out the audience. There's more chiefs here than braves."

Clare looked around the room and shrugged. "No one cares about poetry anymore. See these people—they're all here for their own reasons, but I bet grooving on verse isn't one of them."

"Then why do you do this, Clare?"

"I can't ask myself that. I just do it. Some people paint, others do stained glass, some fuck—I write poems." She began packing away the leftover cheese and crackers. "I'm proud of my poems, Jason. Even if ultimately they have no more value than a child's balloon, I can't worry about that. I know you make fun of us. I know you think we *suck*, but I don't care." She lit a Virginia Slim and blew the smoke out of the corner of her mouth. "If I didn't have my poetry, I'd be even crazier than I am now."

"No, Clare. You won me over tonight. You definitely don't suck."

"Such high praise. I *don't suck*."

"What I mean is you were great. Your performance was powerful. You should try your stuff with a band, you know, Grateful Dead-like—when they go into their Space jams."

As Jason was carrying a plastic sack of trash out the back door to the dumpster, one of the readers cornered him just before he stepped outside. "Hey Jason," she said, "I've got some hash, but I don't have a pipe."

Hash sounded good to Jason. It might mellow me out, he thought. "Me neither, but I'll bet Clare has one. I'm sure she smokes. Wait here and I'll see."

Clare was standing in the gallery, talking with a few people. Jason walked up beside her and whispered, "Clare, I need to ask you something," as he pulled her away from the group. "Do you have a pipe I can borrow for a little while?"

She scrunched up her face and looked at Jason with half-closed eyes. "What are you *doing* asking me *that*? How *dare* you ask me *that*?"

"I'm sorry," Jason said. "It's just that we *really* need one."

Her features softened. She pulled something from her purse and slipped it into his hand. It was wrapped in a handkerchief.

"Here," she said. "But I need this back. Tonight. Make sure I get this back *tonight*. OK?"

"Thanks, Clare."

"OK?"

"OK. Sure. Don't worry. You will."

Jason walked back to where the girl with the hash was waiting. "All right. I got one." He unwrapped the cloth and found a fresh, unused syringe.

"What the fuck!?" Jason exclaimed. Clare had talked about how she liked to do speed, but he never dreamed that she shot it up. And why did she give me a syringe when I asked her for a pipe? he asked himself.

"Hey—I'm not into this," Hash Girl said, shoving the hash back into her purse. "I'm outta here." She walked out the back door with a half-empty bottle of Burgundy hooked around her index finger.

Jason stood alone, clasping the syringe in his hands so that no one would see it. The idea of shooting up—inserting a needle into his vein—made him queasy. And yet, standing here with the syringe cradled in his hands, he became curious. He slowly pulled the plunger out and pushed it back in, feeling the resistance. He used his index finger to tap the plastic cover that protected the needle. He could never shoot himself up. He didn't like the sight of blood, especially his own. But he couldn't help wonder what it was like.

So they call this a *pipe*, Jason thought, as he carefully rewrapped it and slipped it into his pants pocket. That actually makes sense. I'd better get out of this psychedelic monkey suit and make it to Clare's party.

Clare's apartment was crammed with people Jason had never seen before. A group sat cross-legged in a circle on the living room floor, passing joints, saying little. As someone got up, someone else took their place. In other rooms people stood, holding bottles of beer and talking about how high they were, how high they had been at some point, or how high they were going to get. A mural that looked suspiciously like one of Ginzo's creations covered an entire wall. The place smelled like a bar—if bars allowed pot smoking.

Jason found Clare in the kitchen and handed her the wrapped syringe. He spoke quietly into her ear. "Thanks, Clare, but I didn't use this. When I asked for a pipe I meant to smoke with."

"Well then, you should have asked for a *pot* pipe."

"*This* what you should be writing about, Clare," he said, pointing to the partygoers. "—that hiking in the woods and climbing mountains, marveling at the oneness of creation, is good, but it's been done to death. Gary Snyder had the last word on that. The real poems are right here."

"Yeah," she replied, "but you have to be careful. You can

get in trouble for putting that kind of stuff out there. If it's fiction, nobody cares, but if you say it's real, it'd damn well better be some motherfucking morality tale—'How I Got Off Drugs and Became a Productive Citizen Again' or some fairy story like that."

"I'm curious about this whole shooting up thing. I've never done it myself—"

"No shit."

"—but I'm curious. *Very* curious. Do you think you could shoot me up so I can see what it's like?"

Clare didn't hesitate. "Sure, if you want. But I've got to shoot up first. Come with me."

She shut the door to her bedroom, sat down at her desk and pulled out some powder wrapped in aluminum foil, a spoon, a ball of cotton and a book of matches. She prepared her fix, wrapped a piece of tubing around her arm, and inserted the needle. She then pushed the plunger in a little bit and retracted it. Blood appeared in the syringe.

"What's that?" Jason asked.

"I'm making sure I got the vein. It's called aspiration. I used to be a nurse's aide. I've given plenty of shots. I know what I'm doing. Shut up now."

She slowly pushed the plunger in all the way, closed her eyes, inhaled and then exhaled loudly. "Oh yes. Oh yes *yes* oh *baby*—YES!!! she whispered as she removed the needle and tie from her arm. Her voice became louder. "*That's* what mama needed. Yes, YES—*YES!*" She closed her eyes and threw her head back.

She was in her own world and out of her mind and in no shape to shoot anyone up—whether she'd been trained to or not. What scared Jason the most was how much she had wanted the shot. How she had lost all control. I'm never going to do that, he promised himself. If I could make Sophie feel like that, I'd be the world's greatest lover.

"Thanks, Clare," Jason said. "I've got to go now, but I'll catch you later, OK?"

Clare nodded.

Shit, Jason thought. That was close. If she had shot me up first, who knows what would have happened.

169

When Jason returned to his apartment, he noticed that Sophie hadn't come home yet. No problem, he thought, as he curled up in his favorite chair. Those rehearsals always run late. I've got a good thing going with Sophie. Maybe it's time we made some sort of *official* commitment.

19

THE ROSE GARDEN
OF FORKING PATHS

At breakfast the next morning, Sophie's first words to Jason were "Sweetie, I have something to tell you."

He set his coffee cup down, leaned back and rested both hands on the table.

"I was worried when I came home so late last night and found you crashed in the living room. I couldn't hardly wake you to get you to bed."

Here it comes, he thought.

"I think we've been drifting too far from each other," she said. "I was so busy with my work, I missed your poetry reading—"

Good thing, too, Jason thought. He wrapped his hand around the mug.

"—and lots of other things. But what I need to tell you is that my old boyfriend is in town. You remember—I told you about him."

Jason picked up the mug.

"I wasn't answering his letters—I didn't know what to say or how to say it. He finally came out here and caught up with me—I'm not sure how—last night at the theater."

Jason took a sip of his coffee, curled his toes inward, squeezed them, and set the mug down again.

"The moment we saw each other, we both knew it was over. He looked so sad, like a little boy drenched in rain. But it's over now. He won't be back. This is a good thing for us."

Jason dug his tablespoon into his oatmeal. "I didn't know that you didn't know it was over."

"It's just you and me now, Sweetie. There's no one else. It's just you and me . . . Either that or I'm all alone here. Just me and that little theater we all have to scrounge for day and night just to keep the doors open. *And*—I don't think there's an *eligible* bachelor in the bunch."

A slight smile appeared at the corners of her mouth and Jason knew she was trying to lighten the mood.

The morning light cast her face in half shadow as she sat before him with no make-up, speechless and spent in that tattered robe, amid costumes scattered or hanging limply on rolling metal racks, her heart tender and unguarded.

Jason stood up, walked around the table and stood behind her. He rested his hands lightly on her shoulders and began massaging them. I'm almost twenty-seven, he told himself. I'm all set to start at the university next semester. And I almost fucked up in a big way last night. Maybe it's time to not let every stray breeze blow me where it will.

Sophie stood up and faced him. "Jason Giovanni Jones— how long have we been together?"

Oh oh. She's calling me by my full name. How long *have* we been together? He couldn't say.

She opened her robe and pressed her body gently against his. That petite pixie frame, those green eyes camouflaged by those oversized eyeglass frames, overpowered him. They held each other tight.

Jason felt the postcard in his shirt pocket rub against his chest. All it said was: "Meet me at the Saturday Market the first Saturday morning after you get this. I have something of yours." For a signature, there was a drawing of a flute with musical notes coming out of it.

You'll always have my heart, Flute Girl, he had thought when he first read it, but now he wasn't so sure. Would a life with Sophie and a couple of rug rats be so bad? She'd never say it, but I know that's what she wants.

He removed her glasses and pulled her to the floor.

Afterwards, Sophie pressed her palms to his chest, pushed him back far enough to look into his eyes and said, "Just about two years. That's how long." She nestled her head on his shoulder. "Maybe it's time to define our relationship a little bit more. Maybe it's time to . . . Just think about it. She stood up and closed her robe. "Did you get enough to eat?" she asked.

Jason sat back down at the table. The food was cold. "I guess I did," he replied.

How did Jenny get this address? Jason asked himself. She probably got it from Scratchy. I wonder what he told her. Probably not much. He stays out of other people's business. Good thing I got the mail. I should have kept my PO box. That's a conversation I'm glad I didn't have to have.

Later that morning, Jason walked to the edge of the Saturday Market where Jenny had had her flute stand. He knew this was where she'd be. He heard the evanescent melody before he saw her. She was wearing a white cotton dress, her silver flute surrounded by a flurry of notes. The silver of his St. Jude medal around her neck reflected the sunlight back toward him like a secret handshake. She looked half materialized in the morning mist, not fully linked to the earth. Her long blonde hair shone in the noonday sun, flirting with a gentle breeze. Their eyes met. She lowered the flute and dropped her hands to her side, palms out. Jason ran to her. "Jenny!?" he cried.

She pulled him tight against her. They kissed.

"Jason—" She gasped for breath. "Jason . . . It's been too too long." She smiled that half smile of hers and bit the tip of her tongue.

Jason opened his mouth to speak, but Jenny spoke first. "Jay—I told you I'd be back. I came all the way back up here to tell you something—ask you something. It's too much for a letter or phone call. I needed to see you. But there's time for that." She packed away her flute and dropped it into the white cotton bag slung over her shoulder. "C'mon. Spend a little time with me first." She took his hand.

Jason felt her radiance. He still loved her with a love that belonged to another world, another dimension. How could time and distance have so easily dulled his memory? Jason walked in a daze, inhaling her scent and marveling at her long blonde hair, which the breeze would occasionally blow softly across his cheek. It seemed like seconds or days—Jason couldn't be sure which—since they had clasped hands earlier this morning at the Saturday Market. Now, he realized, they were in the Rose Garden. Twenty minutes. It couldn't have been more than that. He hadn't consciously headed here, but if he had, he couldn't have made a better choice.

They sat on a bench, amidst the delicate fragrance of roses, listening to the river roll in the distance. Jenny was the first to speak. "I'm OK now. I think I have this thing beat. I don't want to say it too loud, but I'm better now. Better than any time that you've known me. I wanted my hair to grow back out before you saw me again, as a sign of my strength."

And transcendent beauty, Jason thought. He couldn't look away. Her eyes, her lips, the way the light played across her face . . . It took great effort for him to speak. "Why don't we sit over there on those rocks by the river?"

They climbed down into an alcove of trees, level with the river. Amidst the sound of the water and the cars on the freeway bridge, Jenny said, "Jay, it's been a long time, I know. You've probably got a new life, a new girl. I don't know. And I don't need to know. I just have to ask you something. I don't want you to answer now, I just want you to hear the question."

"Now *you* be quiet," Jason whispered. "I want to remember this moment forever." He kissed her.

"Jay—it's been a long time for something else too. You're the last man I've been with. The only man I want to be with. I know it seems like a long time, but I was out of it for a long time too—you remember. Take it easy with me, Love-light."

They made love on the ground, her cotton dress unbuttoned down the front. Jason felt like they were making love on a cloud, a love that knows no time and finds no expression in words.

When the time for words returned, Jenny removed the silver medal from her neck and placed it around his. She said, "I have no right to ask you this, but I'd like you to maybe come live with me in California. There's a lot you don't know about me, but there's nothing you don't know that would prevent you from being with me." She looked past Jason at the river. "Except that I might not be able to have babies. But you could probably guess that. I don't know for sure, but I can't imagine it's possible after everything I've been through. And you deserve babies of your own."

"I don't care about that."

"Don't say that. Someday you may run into me and pull out a wallet full of pictures and say, 'See what a beautiful creature I've created.'" She inhaled silently. Jason knew only by the movement of her chest. "And . . ." she said, "I don't know how much time I have left on this earth."

"No one knows that."

Jenny tensed her lower lip as if reaching for a high note on her flute. "You know what I mean . . . The rest of my story is mundane. You met my mother. You can draw your own conclusions about that."

"I like your mother."

"I know. She likes you. She likes you a lot more than . . . Well anyway, she likes you. That's saying something. She doesn't like anyone. And . . ." She smiled a quick smile and looked down at the ground. "I'm actually more of a musician than my wooden flutes may have led you to believe. I just got on as a flautist with the San Diego Symphony. I auditioned just to see if I could still play at that level and I got on as an alternate."

"I knew you were good. I just didn't know how good."

"Anyway, rehearsals start next week. I had to come up and try and see you before then. Now I'm asking you to come down there and be with me."

She ran her fingers down his spine and Jason gasped for

breath. "I will," he said. "But I can't . . . I will if I can . . . I mean . . ."

"Hey, I know you can't just throw your guitar in your backseat and follow me down this afternoon. I talked to Scratchy. He said he thought maybe you were going to school. But there are schools in California. There are plenty of schools everywhere. But there's only one of me."

Jason stood up, pulling her up with him. "We've got a lot of catching up to do. Let's grab something to eat at the Zoo."

"No," she said, buttoning her dress up the front. "I don't want to influence you on this any more than I already have. You need to make this decision alone. Listen to your heart in the silence. *Really* listen. If this is to be my last memory of you, I don't want to tarnish it with goodbyes. I don't want you to say anything you don't mean. I don't want you to say anything that isn't true."

She reached into her bag and pulled out a business card from the symphony. "I wrote my address and number on the back. Call first or just show up and surprise me—it doesn't matter which. But if you do come, come soon—don't keep me wondering."

They climbed up the embankment and stood near the bike path leading back to the Rose Garden.

She pressed her lips to his for what seemed like an eternity. A spray of gentle rain enveloped them.

"Maybe I'm just a silly girl in love, but I love you, Jason."

"I love you too, Jennifer."

"Maybe that's all that we get out of this life. Maybe it's enough. I know it's a lot more than some people ever get. I'll see you in the future," she said, as she turned and disappeared into the scent of thousands of roses.

"And not the pasture," Jason whispered, as he welled up with tears that he willed not to leave his eyes.

That evening, Jason and Sophie were lounging on the sofa, drinking chamomile tea, and she asked, "Do you know what you want to major in at the university?"

"Huh? What?"

"I *said*—What do you want to study when you go to the

university this fall? What's the matter with you? You've been distracted all day."

"I know. You gave me a lot to think about this morning and I'm thinking about it. I don't know. Folklore, I guess."

"I'm sorry, Jason. It's just that I want to be closer to you. I didn't mean to discombobulate you. It's just that I, I haven't been as close to you as I could have been—should have been—these past few months. And I want to make it up to you."

"No. You're great. Just let me sleep on all this. As you like to say—we need to do this right. I'll be OK in the morning. I promise."

"Well, you can't just take folklore. I think you should consider anthro—anthropology—as your major. It's a wide-open study of humanity and you could get into culture or specific parts of culture such as music or folktales. You'll have lots of options."

"You take such good care of me. And you're so smart. You could be an advisor."

She snorted. "I certainly know enough about the university. My dissertation title was 'From Muscle Shoals to Motown: Minstrelsy in Girl-Group Garb During the Post World War II Northern Migration' and it took me three years to complete. I thought I'd never finish it. I'll tell you what—for now, I'll be *your* advisor. I believe in you, Sweetie."

She playfully kicked at Jason. He grabbed her feet and pulled them to his. He tried to push them away with all his might, but she held steady. "I love it when you get all intellectual on me. You know how to ground me."

That night in bed, Jason sank into the recesses of his oceanic heart and fought against the winds trying to twist him skyward. But he held on, confident they would not dislodge him.

When he opened his eyes to the morning sun on the heliotrope curtains and felt the counterclockwise rotation of the ceiling fan, he knew his journey was far from over.

I didn't come out West to settle down here like this, to just transplant myself, he thought. I could have stayed back East for that.

Jenny blew through here for a reason. I don't know where I'll end up, but she's the key to me getting me there. She's my conductor on this voyage.

Let's face it—I'll never love Sophie the way she deserves to be loved. Just that I'm even thinking about bailing out tells me all I need to know.

I need to throw my stuff in the Galaxie and go. I need to go and I need to go now. If I don't, I might not ever get out of here. I gotta go with the flow. It'll be smooth sailing, if I go with the flow.

20

FURTHER

Jason **threw a few changes of clothes** into the back-seat of his Galaxie, held Sophie in a long embrace and kissed her goodbye. She said she believed him when he told her he wanted one last road trip to destinations unknown before buckling down at the university. But the way she had so gently rested her palm on his cheek . . . Maybe she already knew.

The tires rolling on the asphalt lulled him into thoughtfulness. He had all the angles covered. He had a fallback position if things with Jenny didn't work out. School was another three months off. His guitar and notebooks were safely stashed in the trunk—he hadn't let Sophie see him take those. Maybe he'd return to Emerald, but no matter what happened, this was a way to gently break from her.

Jason was still in Oregon, barely three hours out of Emerald. The wind flapping through the open windows filled the car with the scent of the freshly sawn wood from the mill on the outskirts of Sevens, a small logging town big enough to have separate buildings for the post office, gas station and general store.

He had never seen so much timber in one place. Planks were piled high on pallets and logs were arranged in pyramids that looked like giant stacks of firewood. Tractors with huge claws moved logs onto conveyor belts and massive saws buzzed over the racket of steel rollers and wheels. The operation must have covered more than four square city blocks. You could build an entire town with the lumber here, he thought.

Suddenly the Galaxie began to sputter and shimmy. Dark smoke rose from the engine compartment. Jason grabbed the steering wheel with both hands. He knew enough to kill the engine, put the car in neutral and coast toward the only gas station in town. The mechanic said it'd probably take a couple of days to fix—if he could fix it all. He wouldn't know until the engine cooled and he could dig around in there a bit.

Jason walked to the general store across the street. The overhang that ran the length of it sagged in the middle and the cedar shake on its sides was weathered grey. Two men, whose faces were lined like a roadmap, played checkers outside. Wooden crates filled with empty bottles were stacked out front next to a soda machine. He put in a quarter, pulled out a green bottle of 7-Up and reached into the coin-return slot for his change. It was like stepping back to a time when Elvis scandalized the nation and the Lennon Sisters ruled the airwaves—to a time before the times were a changin', before Jimi torched the national anthem, before LBJ signed the Voting Rights Act into law, and before anyone had tuned in, turned on, and dropped out.

Jason was about to go inside when he heard a familiar voice. "Hey Greenhorn—See you had some car trouble. I saw you talking to that mechanic across the street. He's a good guy, but he won't win any records for speed."

Rainbow. It had to be Rainbow from the treeplanting gig. She's the only one who'd ever called him that. He turned and saw a woman in a backless, yellow cotton dress, her hair tied in a bun, a locket hanging from her neck on a thick silver chain. "Rainbow? You . . ."

"What's the matter Greenhorn? Don't recognize me without my hardhat and twelve-inch boots?"

"No. It's just that . . . Wow. I didn't expect to see you here."

"Summers I sometimes stay with some friends here up

the road. The locals call it *thatdamnhippiecommune*—
Yeah, that's one word. I don't know what a hippie is. It's
just a word someone made up for other people not like
them. And we're definitely not a commune. A bunch of us
share a house on a few acres. We grow our own veggies,
raise some chickens for their eggs and try to be as self-suf-
ficient as possible. But *commune*? Not even close. We have
running water and electricity. We're not *that* primitive. But
to them it's a commune—so as a joke we sometimes call it
that.

"And I like to dress up a little when I come to town so I
don't get shot. You don't exactly blend either. Hang with us
while you're waiting to find out about your car."

They climbed into her Jeep and Rainbow slid a cassette
into the player. A mournful pedal steel filled the air.

"Rainbow—Is that your real name?"

"Yeah. I named myself." She laughed. "Is Jason *your* real
name?" She looked him directly in the eyes. Several seconds
passed. "That's OK. You don't need to answer me. You need
to answer yourself. Who are you, Son of Jay?"

Listen to the river sing sweet songs to sooth my soul . . .

She had to be wearing make-up. The contours of her face
were so graceful, her eyelashes so long. She no longer
looked like she could stare down a bear.

She must have caught him looking. She slowly batted
her eyes, smiled demurely and flexed her arm into a muscle. "I'm all woman. It's hard for a woman to be taken seriously in a man's profession—hell—in a man's *world*. But
that's my problem, not yours. It looks like you've got prob-
lems of your own.

"C'mon Son of Jay—let's hang at the commune for a
while.

River keep on singin' singin' soft and sweetly . . .

"Just call me Jay. I'm my own man. I'm gonna call you
Jeepster 'cause the Jeep suits you."

"Oh no you don't. I worked too hard for my name. Besides, isn't the Jeep too *masculine*?" She fluttered her eyelashes and Jason's heart fluttered. "I might let you call me
Rain. We'll see how it goes. By the way, I have a boyfriend,

so don't get any ideas."

"That's cool. I've got a girlfriend. I think."

Lovers may come and go the river rolls and rolls . . .

Before Jason could say anything more, Rainbow fired up the Jeep and sped out of town. She turned left onto a road marked only with a letter. Driveways were becoming spaced further and further apart and soon no houses were visible from the road. "I'm glad you've got this Jeep," he said. "It makes it a lot easier driving around here. I wouldn't want to get stuck out here."

"This is nothing—watch *this*." Rainbow pulled the Jeep off the road and began turning figure eights in a small clearing near the shoulder, perilously close, Jason thought, to a steep drop-off. "This baby will climb over tree trunks like they're toothpicks." Jason felt around for something to hang on to and flashed on his hands getting crushed if the Jeep were to roll over. "Be careful!" he yelled over the music and noise of the tires and engine.

"It's cool," Rainbow replied, pulling back onto the black-top. "I make my own road with this."

"You make your own road wherever you go," Jason replied.

"Anyway, before I take you anywhere else, I want to show you something. There's some old-growth forest maybe an hour from here you need to see. Because of a lawsuit, the loggers couldn't punch their way into it to fell some really gravy trees. Now it's officially been declared a Wilderness Area, so they'll never be logged."

She turned left onto an unmarked road that looked slightly wider than a driveway to Jason—if a car were to come from the opposite direction, it wouldn't be able to pass unless one of them pulled to the side. After some twenty miles, the road turned to gravel. "This is a long way to go to look at some trees," Jason said.

"You say that now," she replied.

Rainbow pulled her Jeep into a wide spot by the side of the road. It was a sunny day, but very little light reached the ground. Ferns, salal and rhododendron grew among the trees, which were so tall Jason couldn't even begin to estimate their height. Moss hung from the limbs.

"The main trail starts here," Rainbow said as they began hiking. "It's not well marked, so you have to know where to find it."

A smaller trail branched off the main one. At its head, a feather lay on the ground. Rainbow bent down to pick it up. "This is the trail we're meant to take," she said. "The feather is a sign." She held it up for Jason to see. "Isn't this beautiful? It looks like a hawk feather."

She sighed and ran her fingers along its sides. "I have too much junk in my life. I know I do. I'm too attached to things. I need to get rid of all my earthly possessions. I'll just keep my feathers and rocks and sticks."

"And your Jeep, too—right?" Jason replied.

"Don't get technical. You know what I mean. I feel so free out here. How much stuff does anyone really need? If it wasn't for the poison oak, I'd take off all my clothes and run through the forest naked. I think in a past life I was a woods nymph."

She didn't look anything like a nymph to Jason, but he kept that thought to himself.

Rainbow picked up the pace and they hiked quickly, the thin trail twisting sharply upward. Jason hadn't kept track of the trail markers, but he figured they had to have hiked close to three miles beside a creek winding to his left. His breathing became labored and the muscles in his legs began to ache. His eyelids became heavy and he had difficulty holding them open. "I need to rest awhile, Rain," Jason said. "I didn't get much sleep last night. I was saying goodbye to—you know how it is—go on ahead and catch up with me on your way back."

"Suit yourself," Rainbow replied, not even slowing down. She walked quickly out of sight.

Jason hoisted himself up onto a fallen tree. His feet didn't reach the ground. He lay back and closed his eyes.

A cloud passed overhead, the forest went dark and he found himself back in his old insurance company, walking unnoticed on the office floor. Nothing had changed except him, and the change was startling. As he stood before his older self, he at first recognized himself only by the silver and turquoise ring on his finger. He wore no wedding band. A trembling hand pushed a wispy strand of grey hair from his lined face.

Moments later, he saw himself sitting in the living room of a small apartment, resting a whiskey and ginger ale on his belly, staring numbly at the static on a television screen. He wondered whether the figure in the recliner still had his old guitar.

Jason's eyes snapped open and he stared directly into the deep blue sky. In the moments between dream and wakefulness, the silence gave way to the trickle of the creek bouncing off the rocks in three-part harmony. He heard Rainbow walking toward him and swung his feet over the side of the log. He began slipping off and she ran to catch him. "You look like you saw a ghost," she said. "Something you want to tell me?"

Jason rested his hand along the bark of the ancient tree to steady himself, and his fingers almost disappeared into its crevices. The shards of his dream scattered and he was now wide awake. "There's no going back, Rain. There's no going back—to *anything*. The forest doesn't care who you are. It doesn't even *know* who you are. You can only be yourself here. It strips *everything* else away."

Jason inhaled deeply and the words kept flowing: "The forest doesn't care where I work or how much money I've got in my pocket or where I go from here. Where the hell am I running to? I get it now. I'm right here. I've always been right here. I don't need to be in a hurry to get anywhere."

He cupped his hand to his ear. "Do you hear that, Rain? How perfect the creek sounds? I've been out of tune with the flow this whole time. I thought I was going with the flow, but I was really fighting it. Trying to control where it takes me is as useless as trying to paddle upstream with that feather."

Rainbow handed the feather to Jason. "Here—you were meant to have this. You'll know what to do when the time comes."

Jason held the feather above his head, and when he felt no breeze, he placed it in the water and watched it slowly float downstream, briefly resting against a rock, before the current carried it further.

Photo by Adelia Parker Castro

Alex Balogh is a New Jersey native who lived in Oregon during the '70s and '80s. He currently resides in St. Louis but ducks into the Beaver State yearly, preferably during the rainy season. He teaches creative writing and has edited the literary journal *Untamed Ink*.

He is the author of the poetry collection *And Yet*, published by Cool Way Press.

This is his first novel.

ACKNOWLEDGEMENTS:

Thanks to Michael Castro for permission to quote "If Ya Wanna Ride It, Ya Gotta Ride It Like Ya Find It," from his most recent book of poems *How Things Stack Up*, published by Singing Bone Press.

The three lines of song quoted in Chapter 20 are inspired by "Brokedown Palace" by Jerry Garcia & Robert Hunter.

Adelia Parker Castro provided the author photo.

Cover photo of Oregon's Opal Creek Wilderness by Alex Balogh.

Mark Barbour collaborated on the dialogue of the Ponderosa scientists.

THANKS TO:

Mark Barbour, who suggested I try to turn my short story "Rainy Season" into this novel, & who inspired me with the self-publication of his own novel, *The Long Take*.

My first readers: Mark Barbour, Gerald Mozur, Ann Canale, Michael Fetters, María Balogh, Pyra "Lightsword" Intihar, & Michael Castro. Thank you for your belief in this project & your constructive criticism.

Double thanks to Mark & Pyra who went above & beyond the call, and to Joseph B. Dence, who caught the typos lurking in the first printing.

The lawyer and now friend (who may wish to remain anonymous) who helped steer me away from an unfavorable book contract.

The St. Louis publisher with whom contract talks broke down over the release clause. I appreciate that you liked my work enough to offer me a contract.

Matt Love & Nestucca Spit Press in Astoria, Oregon for producing quality books while successfully modeling a sustainable, independent publishing paradigm.

The numerous friends & colleagues I pestered with my punctuation, phrasing & cover art questions. Thanks for your expertise & patience.

So he gave up playing the flute and said goodbye to exalted sentiments and romantic dreams: for every ordinary man, in the ferment of his youth, if only for a day or for a minute, has thought himself capable of boundless passions and noble exploits . . . in the corner of every notary's heart lie the moldering remains of a poet.

Gustave Flaubert

Accidental Destination